EUROPE
AMERICA
ASIA
AFRICA
AUSTRALIA

MP3

出差英文 1000句型

English For Business Travel

瑜凌 編著

國家圖書館出版品預行編目資料

出差英文1000句型 / 張瑜凌編著
-- 二版. -- 新北市 : 雅典文化, 民109.03
面 ; 公分. --(全民學英文 ; 55)
ISBN 978-986-98710-0-6(平裝附光碟片)

1.商業英文 2.會話

805.188 108023411

全民學英文系列 55

出差英文1000句型

編著／張瑜凌
責任編輯／賴美君
美術編輯／王國卿
封面設計／林鈺恆

法律顧問：方圓法律事務所／涂成樞律師

總經銷：永續圖書有限公司
永續圖書線上購物網
www.foreverbooks.com.tw

出版日／2020年03月

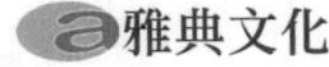

出版社
22103 新北市汐止區大同路三段194號9樓之1
TEL （02）8647-3663
FAX （02）8647-3660

【序文】

臨時抱佛腳，也能說得一口流利的英文！

「明天就要出國出差了，該如何補救我的英文？」

「明天就要招待外籍客戶，該如何和他們溝通？」

「明天就要出國參加商展，該如何回答各種排山倒海而來的問題呢？」

以上的種種問題，許多職場人士都曾經面臨過，也已經沒有時間找齊所有的書籍資料可供學習，更無法一次備齊所有的資料，況且在出差的期間，凡事簡單迅速、凡事克難的情況下，您還有多餘的行李空間可以隨身攜帶所有的書本嗎？此時，「出差英文 1000 句型」就替您解決了上述的種種問題。

「出差英文 1000 句型」超過上千句的例句，著重在簡單、好記的特色，更重要的是，集結了所有在出國出差過程中，您所可能面臨的情境，包括搭飛機、住宿、交通、商展、開會、簡報…等，本書一次編錄齊全，讓您輕輕鬆鬆滿足出差期間的所有溝通需求。

「出差英文 1000 句型」也強調順口好用的溝通技巧，不以艱澀的英文單字為例句範本，讓您能夠在出差的前一天，甚至是在飛機上，也能順利的背誦、運用。

此外，「出差英文 1000 句型」還提供真人伴讀MP3，讓您一句一句練習。只要跟著MP3多唸幾遍，您的口語英文能力一定會突飛猛進！

俗話說，「臨陣磨鎗，不亮也光」，「出差英文1000 句型」提供的英文情境例句，不但能讓你學習迅速，而且實用性高，讓您出差期間，能夠攻無不克、戰無不勝，順利完成出差任務！

Chapter 1 在機場

Chapter 2 在海關

Chapter 3 在飛機上

Chapter 4 旅館住宿

Chapter 5 交通

Chapter 6 電話聯絡

Chapter 7 拜訪客戶

Chapter 8 接待客戶

Chapter 9 舉行會議

Chapter 10 作簡報

Chapter 11 參加商展

Chapter 12 回國

EUROPE
AMERICA
ASIA
AFRICA
AUSTRALIA

Chapter 1

在機場

MP3 001

Lesson 1

機票

I would like a nonstop [1] flight.
我要訂直達的班機。

I would like to book [2] a round-trip [3] ticket.
我要訂一張來回機票。

I would like to book two seats [4].
我要訂兩張機票。

How much is the airfare [5]?
機票多少錢？

I would like to know the airfare.
我想要知道票價。

What's the one way fare?
單程票價是多少錢？

What's the fare from Taipei to Tokyo?
從台北到東京票價是多少錢？

Please tell me the cheapest way.
請告訴我最實惠的方法。

Phrase List

Phrase List

★**would like** + 名詞　我要

I would like a cup of coffee.

我要一杯咖啡。

★**book a ticket** 訂票

I'd like to book a ticket.

我要訂一張票。

★**how much** + 不可數名詞　...是多少

How much is the airfare?

機票多少錢？

Word Bank

Word Bank

1. **nonstop** *a.* 直達的、不停的
2. **book** *v.* 預訂
3. **round-trip** 回程
4. **seat** *n.* 座位
5. **airfare** *n.* 飛機票價

MP3 002

Lesson 2

行程

I want to make a reservation [1] from Taipei to Dallas.

我要預約從台北到達拉斯的機票。

I'd like to book the first flight [2] to Tokyo for May 1st.

我想預訂五月一日到東京的最早航班。

Do you fly [3] to New York on September 2nd?

你們有九月二日到東京的班機嗎？

Do you fly from Taipei to Tokyo on September 2nd?

你們有九月二日從台北到紐約的班機嗎？

I want to fly to Chicago on the 1st of September.

我想要在九月一日飛芝加哥。

I'd like to book a nonstop flight from New York to Paris.

我想預訂從紐約到巴黎的直達航班。

I'm thinking of flying from Paris to Seattle on May 1st and from Seattle to Tokyo on May 8th.
我打算五月一日從巴黎到西雅圖，以及五月八日從西雅圖到東京。

Phrase List

★**make a reservation** 預約

I want to make a reservation to Taipei.

我要預約到台北（的機位）。

★**be thinking of** +動名詞 正打算做某事

I am thinking of calling him.

我打算打電話給他。

Word Bank

1. **make a reservation** 預定
2. **flight** *n.* 航班
3. **fly** *v.* 飛行

MP3 003

Lesson 3

訂機位／取消機位／變更機位

I would like to book two seats from Taipei to New York on August 25th.
我要訂兩個人八月廿五日從台北到紐約的機票。

I would prefer a morning flight.
我偏好早上的班機。

I would like to book flight 803 on August 25th.
我要訂八月廿五日的803班次。

I would like the 9 am one.
我要九點的那一個班次。

通常你會聽到對方這麼說：

◆There's a flight at 9 am and one at 11 am.
早上九點有一班，還有一班是十一點。

◆Which would you prefer?
您想要哪一個班次？

I want to cancel my reservation.
我想取消我的訂位。

I would like to change my flight.
我想變更我的班機。

Phrase List

★**prefer+**名詞　偏好某事

I prefer the red one.

我偏好紅色那個。

★**cancel reservation**　取消預約

I'd like to cancel my reservation.

我想要取消我的訂位。

MP3 004

Lesson 4 航班查詢

Could you please find [1] another flight before it?
請你替我找那一天之前的另一個班機好嗎？

Are there two seats available [2] on the 2 pm flight?
下午兩點起飛的飛機還有兩個空位嗎？

Do you fly to New York on next Monday?
你們有下星期一到紐約的班機嗎？

Could you check the boarding time [3] for me?
你能替我查班機時刻表嗎？

But I can't make it until [4] the 30th of August.
可是我八月卅日前無法成行。

It's Flight 306.
是306號班機。

From Taipei to Seattle.
從台北到西雅圖。

Phrase List

★**Could you please**+原形動詞

能否請你做某事

Could you please write me a note?

能否請你幫我寫一張備忘錄？

★**be available** 有空閒的

Mr. White is available now.

懷特先生現在有空。

★**make it** 能夠做某事

Can you make it on time?

你能準時做到嗎？

Word Bank

1. **find** *v.* 尋找
2. **available** *a.* 可用的、有效的
3. **boarding time** 班機時刻
4. **until** *prep.* 直到…為止

MP3 005

Lesson 5

特定航班

I would like to reschedule [1] the flight at 4 pm.
我想把班機改成下午四點的那班飛機。

I would like to change [2] the flights for the same date.
我想改成同一天的其他航班。

I would like to reconfirm [3] my seat on the 10 am flight to Seattle for October 7th.
請再確認一下我預訂的十月七日上午十點飛西雅圖的航班。

I'm looking for a flight from Tokyo to Paris on July 3rd.
我正在找七月三日從東京到巴黎的航班。

I would prefer [4] a morning flight.
我偏好上午的班機。

I want to leave on next Wednesday.
我想要在下星期三離開。

I'm planning to depart[5] on September 1st or 2nd.

我想九月一日或二日出發。

Phrase List

★**reschedule the flight** 更改班機行程

Would you like to reschedule the flight?

你要更改班機行程嗎？

★**look for+**名詞 尋找某物

I'm looking for a black coat

我正在找一件黑色外套。

★**plan to+**原形動詞　計畫做某事

I plan to travel around the world.

我計劃要環遊世界。

Word Bank

1. **reschedule** *v.* 重新安排日期
2. **change** *v.* 更改
3. **reconfirm** *v.* 再確認
4. **prefer** *v.* 偏好
5. **depart** *v.* 起程、出發

MP3 006

Lesson 6

辦理報到

Where may I check in[1] for United Airlines Flight 706?

我應該在哪裡辦理聯合航空706班機的登機手續？

Can I check in now?

我現在可以辦理登機嗎？

Can I check in for CA Flight 546?

我可以辦理CA546班機登機嗎？

Check-in, please.

我要辦理登機。

I would like to check in.

我要辦理登機。

Here is my passport[2] and visa[3].

這是我的護照和簽證。

Do you need my ticket[4]?

需要我的機票嗎？

What time should I have to be at the airport?
我應該什麼時候到機場？

Phrase List

★**check in**　辦理報到

When can I check in?

我什麼時候可以辦理報到？

★**here is**+名詞　這是…

Here is my ticket.

這是我的車票。

Word Bank

1. **check in**　辦理登機
2. **passport**　*n.*　護照
3. **visa**　*n.*　簽證
4. **ticket**　*n.*　機票

MP3 007

Lesson 7

機位

May I have a window seat [1]?

我可以要靠窗戶的座位嗎？

I don't want the aisle seat [2].

我不要走道的位子。

I want an aisle seat, please.

我想要一個走道的位子。

I want the first class seat [3].

我想要頭等艙的座位。

Is it an aisle seat?

這是靠走道的座位嗎？

I would like to reconfirm a flight.

我要再確認機位。

I'd like to reconfirm a flight for Mr. White.

我想替懷特先生再確認機位。

Phrase List

★**may I**+原形動詞　我是否可以…

May I have a blanket?

我可以要一張毯子嗎？

★**reconfirm a flight**　再確認機位

I'm trying to reconfirm a flight reservation on Air China.

我嘗試要再確認搭乘中國航空的預定班機。

Word Bank

1. **window seat**　靠窗座位
2. **aisle seat**　走道座位
3. **first class seat**　頭等艙座位

MP3 008

Lesson 8 行李托運

I have baggage [1] to be checked.
我有行李要托運。

I have two suitcases [2].
我有兩件行李箱。

They are all hand-carry [3] bags.
這些都是手提(上飛機)的袋子。

How much baggage can I take on a China flight?
搭乘中國航空的班機我可帶多少行李？

Can I carry this bag with me?
我可以隨身帶這個袋子嗎？

Shall I put my baggage here?
我可以把我的袋子放這裡嗎？

How much is the extra charge [4]?
超重費是多少？

What are your charges for excess [5] baggage?
你們的行李超重費是多少？

Phrase List

★**put shtg.+here** 將某物置於此處

Can I put my books here?

我可以把我的書放在這裡嗎？

You may put your bags here.

你可以把你的袋子放在這裡。

Phrase List

Word Bank

1. **baggage** *n.* 行李
2. **suitcase** *n.* 小型旅行箱
3. **hand-carry** 手提的
4. **extra charge** 超重費
5. **excess** *a.* 過量的、額外的

Word Bank

MP3 009

Lesson 9

行李提領

Where can I get my baggage?
我可以在哪裡提領行李？

Is this the baggage claim area[1] from USA Airlines 561?
這是美國航空 561 班機的行李提領處嗎？

Can I get my baggage now?
我可以現在提領我的行李嗎？

Could you help me get my baggage down?
你可以幫我把我的行李拿下來嗎？

Where can I get a baggage cart[2]?
我可以在哪裡拿到行李推車？

Where is the baggage cart?
哪裡有行李推車？

Excuse me, sir, that is my baggage.
先生，抱歉，那是我的行李。

This is not my baggage.
這不是我的行李。

Phrase List

★**help sbdy.+原形動詞**　幫助某人做某事

Let me help you clean it up.

讓我幫你清乾淨。

Would you help me move this box?

可以請你幫我搬這個箱子嗎？

Phrase List

Word Bank

1. **claim area**　行李提領處
2. **baggage cart**　行李推車

Word Bank

Lesson 10

行李遺失

I don't see my baggage.
我沒有看見我的行李。

I can't find my baggage. What can I do?
我找不到我的行李。我應該怎麼辦？

One of my bags hasn't come.
我的一件行李沒有出來。

I may have lost my baggage.
我可能遺失我的行李了。

Did you see my red bag?
你有看見我的紅色袋子嗎？

Where is the Lost Baggage Service?
行李遺失申報處在哪裡？

Do you know where the Lost Baggage Service is?
你知道行李遺失申報處在哪裡嗎？

通常你會聽到對方這麼說：

◆May I see your baggage tag?

我可以看一下你的行李牌嗎？

◆Please fill out this claim form.

請填這張申訴表格。

Phrase List

★**one of+**複數可數名詞　其中一個...

One of my books is gone.

我的一本書不見了。

★**do you know+where**子句

你是否知道...在哪裡？

Do you know where David is?

你知道大衛在哪裡嗎？

★**fill out**　填寫

How should I fill out this form?

我要怎麼填寫這張表格？

MP3 011

Lesson 11

登記行李遺失

I think two pieces[1] of my baggage have been lost.

我覺得我的兩件行李遺失了。

It is a medium-sized[2], and it is black.

中等尺寸，黑色的。

通常你會聽到對方這麼說：

◆Can you tell me the features of your baggage?

你能形容一下你行李的外觀嗎？

How long will you find out?

你們要多久才會找到？

What if you couldn't find my baggage?

萬一你們找不到我的行李怎麼辦？

Will you inform[3] me as soon as you find them?

你們找到它們的時候，可以立刻通知我嗎？

Please deliver[4] my baggage to this address[5].

請將我的袋子送到這個地址。

Phrase List

★**have been lost** 已經遺失

One of my hats has been lost.

我的一頂帽子遺失了。

★**find out** 尋找

How did you find it out?

你們怎麼找到它的？

★**what if** 假使、萬一

What if we couldn't finish it in time?

萬一我們無法如期完成該怎麼辦？

Word Bank

1. **piece** *n.* 一件、一個
2. **medium-sized** 中等尺寸
3. **inform** *v.* 運送通知、告知
4. **deliver** *v.* 運送
5. **address** *n.* 地址

MP3 012

Lesson 12

出境登機

I am on a USA Airlines flight.
我要搭乘美國航空公司。

What time will boarding [1] start?
什麼時候開始登機？

What's the boarding time [2]?
登機時間是什麼時候？

Is the flight on time [3]?
班機準時起飛嗎？

Excuse me, where should I board [4]?
請問，我應該到哪裡登機？

Where is the boarding gate?
登機門在哪裡？

I don't know where I should board.
我不知道我應該在哪裡登機。

I think I am at the wrong gate.
我想我走錯登機門了。

Phrase List

★**what time**+倒裝句　什麼時間...？

What time did he call you back?

他什麼時間回你電話的？

★**on time** 準時

Will you be there on time?

你會準時到達嗎？

Phrase List

Word Bank

1. **boarding** *n.* 上船(或火車、飛機等)
2. **boarding time** 登機時間
3. **on time** 準時
4. **board** v. 登機

Word Bank

MP3 013

Lesson 13

轉機

Where can I get information on a connecting flight [1]?

我可以到哪裡詢問轉機的事？

How should I transfer [2]?

我要如何轉機？

How do I transfer to Washington?

我要如何轉機到華盛頓？

I am in transit [3].

我要轉機。

I am in transit to Paris.

我要轉機到巴黎。

I am connecting [4] with CA651.

我要轉搭CA651 班機。

I would like a stop-over flight.

我要訂需要轉機的班機。

I would like a stop-over flight to Los Angeles.
我要訂到洛杉磯的轉機班機。

I prefer to stop over in Hong Kong.
我比較喜歡在香港轉機。

Phrase List

★**information on+**名詞　有關...的資訊

I had received information on the accident.

我已經收到這個意外的資訊了。

★**stop over**　中途停留

I'd prefer to stop over in Tokyo.

我比較喜歡在東京轉機。

Word Bank

1. connecting flight 轉機班機

2. transfer *v.* 轉機、轉車

3. transit *n.* 過境

4. connect *v.* 連結

MP3 014

Lesson 14

過境

How long will we stop here?

我們會在這裡停留多久？

How long is the stopover [1]?

過境要停留多久？

May I leave [2] my baggage in the plane?

我可以把行李留在飛機上嗎？

I am a transit passenger [3] for Flight UA356.

我是要搭乘美國航班356號的轉機乘客。

I am continuing [4] on to Washington.

我要繼續前往華盛頓。

機場廣播：

☑Ladies and gentlemen, may I have your attention please: American Airlines flight number 657 is now leaving for New York.

各位先生小姐，請注意：美國航空公司657班機即將離境前往紐約。

☑All passengers please come forward to the departure area for boarding.

所有乘客，請到出境室登機。

☑All passengers please board now.
各位乘客開始登機。

☑Attention please: Passengers to New York on American Airlines Flight 624, please board through gate 12.
請注意：搭乘美國航空班機624號前往紐約的旅客，請由十二號登機門登機。

☑Attention please: Due to bad weather, all flights from New York to Paris will be delayed.
請注意：因為惡劣的天氣，所有由紐約前往巴黎的班機將延誤起飛/到達。

Word Bank

1. **stopover** *n.* 中途停留、過境
2. **leave** *v.* 放置
3. **passenger** *n.* 乘客
4. **continue** *v.* 繼續

Word Bank

MP3 015

Lesson 15 兌換貨幣

Where is the currency [1] exchange [2]?
貨幣兌換處在哪裡？

Can I exchange money here?
我可以在這裡兌換錢幣嗎？

Could you change this into [3] dollars?
你可以把這個兌換為美元嗎？

I want to exchange money into Taiwan dollar.
我想要兌換成台幣。

通常你會聽到對方這麼說：

◆What currency do you want to convert from?
你想要用哪一種貨幣兌換？

I'd like to exchange some U.S. dollars to German Marks.
我要把一些美金兌換成德國馬克。

Could you cash [4] a traveler's check [5]?
你可以把旅行支票換成現金嗎？

Phrase List

★**exchange money** 兌換貨幣

When you exchange money, you will receive a receipt.

當你兌換貨幣時，你會收到一張收據。

★**change into** 兌換幣值

Please change Taiwan dollars into dollars.

請把台幣兌換為美元。

Phrase List

Word Bank

1. **currency** *n.* 貨幣
2. **exchange** *v.* 兌換
3. **change into** 兌換為
4. **cash** *v.* 兌換為現金
5. **traveler's check** 旅行支票

Word Bank

MP3 016

Lesson 16

兌換成零錢

Could you give me some small change [1] with it?

你能把這些兌換為零錢嗎？

Would you please break [2] this 100 U.S. dollar bill [3]?

能請您將一百元美金換成零錢嗎？

通常你會聽到對方這麼說：

◆How much do you want to exchange?

你想兌換多少？

Can you make me change for a ￡5 note?

五英鎊的鈔票你能找得開嗎？

Can you change a dollar for ten dimes?

你能把一美元換成十個一角的銀幣嗎？

I want to break this 200 dollars into 4 twenties, 3 tens and the rest in coins.

我想要將兩百元兌換成四張二十元、三張十元，剩下的是零錢。

Could you include [4] some small change?

可以包括一些零錢嗎？

Phrase List

★**small change** 零錢

Please give me small change to tip the bell-boy.

請給我一些零錢給服務生當小費。

★**break** 將錢兌換成小面額

Please break my bill.

請將我的紙鈔換成零錢。

Word Bank

1. **change** *n.* 零錢
2. **break** *v.* 兌開(大額鈔票等)
3. **bill** *n.* 鈔票
4. **include** *v.* 包括、包含

MP3 017

Lesson 17 幣值匯率

I'd like to change NT$10,000 into U.S. dollars.
我要把一萬元台幣換成美金。

How much in dollars is that?
（兑換）美元是多少？

Could you tell me the procedures [1] and the exchange rate [2] for today?
你能告訴我手續和今天的匯率嗎？

What's the exchange rate?
匯率是多少？

From U.S. dollars. What is the exchange rate now?
從美金(換成台幣)。現在匯率是多少？

通常你會聽到對方這麼說：

◆The exchange rate from U.S. dollar to Taiwan dollar is thirty-four point five.
現在美金兌換成台幣的匯率是卅四點五。

Phrase List

★**tell sobdy. sthg.** 告訴某人某事

Let me tell you the truth.

讓我告訴你事實。

Would you tell me your name?

請您告訴我您的大名。

Phrase List

Word Bank

1. **procedure** *n.* 程序、手續
2. **exchange rate** 匯率

Word Bank

MP3 018

Lesson 18

機場常見問題(一)

Where is the person in charge [1]?
負責的人在哪裡？

Will the flight be delayed [2]?
飛機會誤點嗎？

Are there any other flights available?
還有其他班次可以搭乘嗎？

What time does the Flight 803 arrive [3]?
803 次班機何時抵達？

How much is the airport tax?
機場稅是多少錢？

Where is the travel information counter?
旅遊服務中心在哪裡？

Where should I pay the airport tax?
我應該在哪裡付機場稅？

Is this line for non-residents [4]?
非本國人是在這裡排隊嗎？

Phrase List

★**in charge** 負責

I'd like to speak to the person in charge.

我要和負責人講話。

★**any other**+複數可數名詞

任何其他的某物

Are there any other books available?

還有其他書有賣嗎？

Phrase List

Word Bank

1. **in charge** 負責
2. **delay** *v.* 延遲
3. **arrive** *v.* 到達、到來
4. **non-residents** 非本國人

Word Bank

MP3 019

Lesson 19

機場常見問題(二)

Could you page [1] my child for me?
可以幫我廣播呼叫我的孩子嗎？

Do you have maps [2] of the downtown [3]?
你們有市中心的地圖嗎？

Is there a free city map?
有沒有免費的城市地圖？

Where can I get to Four Seasons Hotel?
我要怎麼去四季飯店？

How much does it cost [4] to downtown by taxi?
坐計程車到市中心要多少錢？

Where should I catch a bus [5]?
我要在哪裡搭公車？

Does anyone here speak Chinese?
這裡有沒有會說中文的人？

I am from Taiwan.
我來自台灣。

Phrase List

★**page** 廣播

Where can I page my child?

我可以在哪裡廣播呼叫我的孩子？

★**get to** 到達某處

How should I get to the police station?

我要怎麼去警察局？

★**by taxi** 搭乘計程車

Can I get there by taxi?

我可以搭計程車到那裡嗎？

★**catch a bus** 搭公車

I need to catch a bus.

我需要去搭公車。

Word Bank

1. page *v.* 廣播叫(人)

2. map *n.* 地圖

3. downtown *n.* 市中心

4. cost *v.* 花費

5. catch a bus 搭乘公車

EUROPE
AMERICA
ASIA
AFRICA
AUSTRALIA

EUROPE
AMERICA
ASIA
AFRICA
AUSTRALIA

Chapter 2

在海關

MP3 020

Lesson 1 證照查驗

This is my passport and visa.
這是我的護照和簽證。

Here you are.
給您。

通常你會聽到對方這麼說：

◆May I see your passport and visa, please?
請給我您的護照和簽證。

I want to stay here for about 8 days.
我大約會在這裡停留八天。

I will stay here for one more week.
我會在這裡留一個多星期。

It's about 3 weeks.
大概三個星期。

通常你會聽到對方這麼說：

◆How long are you going to stay in England?
您要在英國停留多久？

Phrase List

★**stay here for**+天數 在此處停留幾天

We'll stay here for five days.

我們將會在此地停留五天。

I planned to stay here for a week.

我計畫好要在這裡停留一個星期。

Phrase List

MP3 021

Lesson 2 簽證

I have a student visa[1].

我拿學生簽證。

I have a business visa[2].

我拿觀光簽證。

I am with my parents.

我和我父母一起來的。

I am with a travel tour[3].

我是跟團的。

I am alone.

我一個人（來的）。

通常你會聽到對方這麼說：

◆Are you traveling alone?

你自己來旅遊的嗎？

I can't find my visa.

我找不到我的簽證。

Word Bank

1. **student visa** *n.* 學生簽證
2. **business visa** *n.* 觀光簽證
3. **travel tour** 旅行團

MP3 022

Lesson 3
入境原因

It's for business [1].
我是來出差的。

I am here for sightseeing [2]/touring [3].
我來這裡觀光/旅行。

I am here for studies.
我來這裡唸書的。

Just touring.
只是旅遊。

通常你會聽到對方這麼說：
◆What's the purpose of your visit?
你此行的目的是什麼？

I am just passing through [4].
我只是過境。

I am leaving for New York this afternoon.
我今天下午要去紐約。

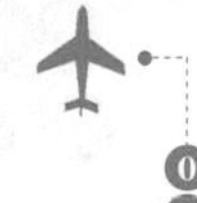

Phrase List

★**for business** 出差

I came here for business.

我來這裡出差。

★**for sightseeing** 觀光

It's for sightseeing.

是來觀光的。

★**for studies** 唸書

I came here for studies.

我來這裡唸書的。

Phrase List

Word Bank

1. **for business** 出差
2. **for sightseeing** 觀光
3. **for touring** 旅遊
4. **pass through** 過境

Word Bank

MP3 023

Lesson 4
通關

通常你會聽到對方這麼說：
◆Place your bag on the belt please.
請將您的袋子放在傳送帶上。

Should I open my baggage?
要我打開我的行李箱嗎？

Just clothes [1], personal belongings [2], and some books.
只是衣物、個人用品和一些書本。

Those medicines [3] are prepared for this tour.
那些藥物是為了這趟旅行而準備的。

They are just some souvenirs [4].
它們只是一些紀念品。

Personal stuff [5].
私人物品。

通常你會聽到對方這麼說：
◆Why do you have them with you?
你為什麼帶這些東西？

Phrase List

★**be prepared for** 為了...而準備的

This special meal is prepared for Indian passengers

這個特別的餐點是為印度乘客準備的。

Word Bank

1. **clothes** *n.* 衣物
2. **belongings** *n.* 攜帶物品
3. **medicine** *n.* 藥
4. **souvenir** *n.* 紀念品
5. **stuff** **n.** 物品

MP3 024

Lesson 5 申報商品

Yes, there are four bottles[1] of wine.

有的，(我)有四瓶酒。

No, I have nothing to declare[2].

沒有，我沒有要申報的物品。

> **通常你會聽到對方這麼說：**
> ◆Do you have anything to declare?
> 有沒有要申報的物品？

No, I don't.

不，我沒有。

> **通常你會聽到對方這麼說：**
> ◆Do you have any prohibited items?
> 有沒有攜帶任何違禁品？

Can't I bring them in?

我不能帶它們進來？

通常你會聽到對方這麼說：

◆I have to confiscate these.

我必須沒收這些東西。

Phrase List

★**have nothing to**+原形動詞

沒有…做某事

We have nothing to say.

我們無話可說。

Word Bank

1. **bottle** *n.* 瓶子
2. **declare** *v.* 申報(納稅品等)

MP3 025

Lesson 6 繳交稅款

How much is the duty[1]?
稅金是多少？

How much is the duty on this?
這個要付多少稅金呢？

通常你會聽到對方這麼說：
◆You have to pay tax for over 100 cigarettes.
你要為超過 100 支的香菸付稅。

How much do I have to pay[2]?
我要付多少錢？

How much did you say?
你說是多少？

Really? I didn't know about it.
真的？我不知道這件事。

How should I pay for it?
我應該要如何付呢？

Phrase List

★**pay for** 付款

Who will pay for this?

誰要買單？

Word Bank

1. **duty** *n.* 稅
2. **pay** *v.* 支付

EUROPE
AMERICA
ASIA
AFRICA
AUSTRALIA

Chapter 3

在飛機上

MP3 026

Lesson 1

尋找機位

Excuse me. Is this 32L?

抱歉，這是32L嗎？

Would you please take me to my seat?

能請你幫我帶位嗎？

I couldn't find my seat.

我找不到我的座位。

Could you show me where my seat is?

你能告訴我我的座位在哪裡嗎？

Would you please take me to my seat?

能請你幫我帶位嗎？

Excuse me. Can you tell me where my seat is?

對不起，你能告訴我我的座位在哪裡嗎？

通常你會聽到對方這麼說：

◆Down this aisle, to your right.

順著走道，在你的右手邊。

◆Go straight ahead, and you will see it on your left.

往前直走，你就會看到在你的左手邊。

◆O.K. It's a window seat on the left.

好的。它是個在左邊靠窗的位子。

Phrase List

★**down to** 向南、向下

You'll see it down this road.

往這條路下去，你就會看見。

★**go straight ahead** 往前直走

Go straight ahead, and you'll see it.

往前直走，你就會看見。

★**on the left/right** 在左/右手邊

You'll see it on the right.

你會在右手邊看見。

MP3 027

Lesson 2

確認機位

Can I change my seat?
我能不能換座位？

Can you switch [1] seats with me?
你能和我換座位嗎？

Excuse me. That's my seat.
抱歉，那是我的位子。

I am afraid this is my seat.
這個恐怕是我的座位。

I am afraid you have my seat.
你恐怕坐了我的座位。

Can we move [2] to the smoking area [3]?
我們能移到吸菸區嗎？

I would like to move to the smoking area.
我想要換位子到吸菸區。

This isn't the non-smoking area [4], right?
這裡不是非吸菸區，是嗎？

Phrase List

Phrase List

★**change seat** 換座位

Can we change our seats?

我們能不能換座位？

★**switch seat** 互換座位

Would you switch seats with my wife?

你能和我的太太互換座位嗎？

★**be afraid** 恐怕

I'm afraid this is wrong.

這個恐怕是錯的。

Word Bank

Word Bank

1. **switch** *v.* 交換
2. **move** *v.* 移動
3. **smoking area** 吸菸區
4. **non-smoking area** 非吸菸區

MP3 028

Lesson 3 起飛前

You can store[1] extra baggage in the overhead[2] cabinet[3].

你可以把多出來的行李放在上方的行李櫃裡。

Excuse me. Where should I put my baggage?

抱歉，我應該把我的行李放哪裡？

I'd better fasten[4] my seat belt[5].

我最好先繫緊我的座位安全帶。

How do I fasten my seat belt?

我要怎麼繫緊安全帶？

機上廣播：

☑Ladies and gentlemen, we will be passing through some turbulence. For your safety, please remain seated and fasten your seat belts.

各位先生小姐，我們即將通過亂流。為了您的安全，請您坐在座位上並繫好您的安全帶。

Phrase List

★**would better+**原形動詞 最好做某事

You'd better change your mind.

你最好改變你的想法。

★**fasten seat belt** 繫緊座位安全帶

You have to fasten your seat belt first.

你必須要先繫緊你的座位安全帶。

Phrase List

Word Bank

1. **store** *v.* 儲藏
2. **overhead** *a.* 在頭頂上的
3. **cabinet** *n.* 櫃子
4. **fasten** *v.* 繫緊
5. **seat belt** 安全帶

Word Bank

MP3 029

Lesson 4

航程

How long does this flight take?
這個航程要多久的時間？

Will we arrive in New York on time?
我們會準時到達紐約嗎？

This is a long flight [1].
這是很長的一段航程。

It's a long flight to France.
到法國是一段很長的旅程。

Are we passing through Japan now?
我們正穿越日本嗎？

How many more hours to Seattle?
到西雅圖還要幾個小時？

I always have jet lag [2] for a few days after a long flight.
通常在一段長程飛行後，我會有幾天時間的時差問題。

Phrase List

★take 花費

The flight will take three hours.

這趟航程要花費三小時。

★pass through 穿越

When did we pass through Japan?

我們什麼時候穿越日本的？

Word Bank

1. **long flight** *n.* 長時間的航程
2. **jet lag** 時差

MP3 030

Lesson 5

與鄰座閒聊

Hi, I am Chris.
嗨，我是克里斯。

You look familiar[1].
你看起來很面熟。

I am Jack. You are?
我是傑克。您的（大名）是？

My name is Sophia. Nice to meet[2] you, Chris.
我是蘇菲亞，很高興認識你，克里斯。

Nice to meet you, too.
(我)也很高興認識你。

Where are you from?
您從哪裡來的？

I am here from London to see my friends.
我來自倫敦，是為了探望我的朋友。

It is nice talking to you.
很高興和你聊天。

Nice talking to you, too.
我也很高興和你聊天。

Phrase List

★**look familiar** 看起來面熟

You look familiar to me.

對我而言，你看起來很面熟。

★**be nice to+**原形動詞　高興去做某事

It's nice to have you here.

真高興有你在這裡。

★**be nice+**動名詞　高興去做某事

It is nice seeing you again.

真高興又看見你。

Word Bank

1. **familiar** *a.* 熟悉的、面熟的
2. **meet** *v.* 遇見

Phrase List
Word Bank

MP3 031

Lesson 6

尋求空服員協助(一)

Would you do me a favor[1]?
你能幫我一個忙嗎？

Would you put this in the overhead bin?
您可以幫我把它放進櫃子裡嗎？

Do you have a Chinese newspaper?
你們有中文報紙嗎？

And may I have a pack of playing cards[2]?
那我可以要一副撲克牌嗎？

I feel cold. May I have a blanket[3]?
我覺得冷。我能要一條毯子嗎？

How do I turn this light on[4]?
我要怎麼打開這燈？

How do I operate[5] this?
這個我要怎麼操作？

Where is the lavatory[6]?
盥洗室在哪裡？

Phrase List

★**do sbdy. a favor** 幫助某人

Please do me a favor, OK?

幫我一個忙好嗎？

★**turn on** 打開（電器、電燈開關等）

Would you turn the stereo on?

可以打開音響嗎？

Phrase List

Word Bank

1. **do sbdy.a favor** 幫某人一個忙
2. **a pack of playing cards** 一副撲克牌
3. **blanket** *n.* 毯子
4. **turn on** 打開
5. **operate** *v.* 操作
6. **lavatory** *n.* 廁所

Word Bank

MP3 032

Lesson 7

尋求空服員協助(二)

Is this vacant[1]?

(廁所)是空的嗎？

通常你會聽到對方這麼說：

◆No, it is occupied.

不是，(裡面)有人。

May I have an earphone[2], please?

可以給我一副耳機嗎？

It doesn't work.

這個不能運轉。

Any Chinese speakers?

有沒有會說中文的人？

Can I recline[3] my seat back now?

我現在可以將椅背往後靠嗎？

What is the local time[4] in the USA?

美國當地時間是幾點鐘？

Word Bank

1. **vacant** *a.* 未被佔用的
2. **earphone** *n.* 耳機
3. **recline** *v.* (座椅)靠背可活動後仰
4. **local time** 當地時間

MP3 033

Lesson 8 尋求空服員協助(三)

What is the temperature [1] in Vancouver?
溫哥華現在溫度多少？

Sorry to bother [2] you.
很抱歉麻煩您了。

Yes, please.
我需要，麻煩你了。

通常你會聽到對方這麼說：

◆Do you need the Customs Form?
您需要海關申報表嗎？

I can arrange[3] it by myself[4]. Thank you.

我可以自己放。謝謝你。

Phrase List

★**be sorry to**+原形動詞　抱歉做某事

I'm sorry to call you so late.

很抱歉這麼晚打電話給您。

★**by one's self**　依靠自己

Can you do it by yourself?

你自己可以做得到嗎？

Word Bank

1. **temperature** *n.* 溫度
2. **bother** *v.* 煩擾、打擾
3. **arrange** *v.* 安排
4. **by myself** 靠自己

MP3 034

Lesson 9
飛機上的餐飲(一)

What time will we have a meal[1] served?

我們幾點用餐？

What do you have?

你們有什麼（餐點）？

通常你會聽到對方這麼說：

◆What would you like for dinner?

晚餐您想吃什麼？

I would like beef, please.

我要吃牛肉，謝謝。

Do you have a vegetarian meal[2]?

你們有素食餐點嗎？

I am still hungry[3].

我還是很餓。

Do you have instant noodles[4]?

你們有泡麵嗎？

May I have a glass of water, please?

我能要一杯水嗎？

Phrase List

★**a glass of**+飲料　一杯（飲料）

Would you like a glass of water?

你想要喝一杯水嗎？

★**by the way**　順便

By the way, are your available this weekend?

順帶一提，你這個週末有空嗎？

Word Bank

1. **meal** *n.* 餐點
2. **vegetarian meal** 素食餐點
3. **hungry** *a.* 飢餓的
4. **instant noodles** 泡麵

MP3 035

Lesson 10

飛機上的餐飲(二)

May I have a glass of orange juice[1]?
我能要一杯柳橙汁嗎？

May I have something to drink?
我能喝點飲料嗎？

I am a little thirsty[2]. Do you have any cold drinks[3]?
我有一點口渴，你們有任何冷飲嗎？

By the way, could you get me some beer[4] too?
你能順便給我一些啤酒嗎？

May I have a glass of hot water? Not too hot, please.
我可以要一杯熱開水嗎？請不要太熱。

Can I have some coffee?
我可以喝一些咖啡嗎？

Coffee, please.
請給我咖啡。

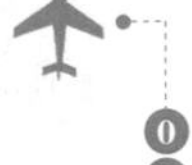

通常你會聽到對方這麼說：

◆And you, sir? Coffee or tea?

先生您呢？咖啡或茶。

May I have some more tea, please?

我能再多要點茶嗎？

Word Bank

1. **orange juice** 柳橙汁
2. **thirsty** *a.* 口乾的
3. **cold drinks** 冷飲
4. **beer** *n.* 啤酒

MP3 036

Lesson 11 不舒服

I don't feel well.
我覺得不舒服。

I feel airsick [1].
我覺得暈機。

I feel like vomiting [2].
我想吐。

I have a headache [3].
我頭痛。

I have a pain [4] here.
我這裡痛。

I have a stomachache [5].
我胃痛。

I have a fever [6].
我發燒了。

I need a doctor.
我需要醫生。

Do you have airsickness bags?

你有嘔吐袋嗎？

Phrase List

★**feel well** 感覺舒服

Do you feel well?

你感覺舒服嗎？

★**feel like**+動名詞 想要做某事

I feel like screaming.

我想尖叫。

Phrase List

Word Bank

1. **airsick** *a.* 暈機的
2. **vomit** *v.* 嘔吐
3. **headache** *n.* 頭痛
4. **pain** *n.* 疼痛
5. **stomachache** *n.* 胃痛
6. **fever** *n.* 發燒

Word Bank

Lesson 12 填寫表格

Will you give me a customs declaration [1]?

能給我一張海關申報單嗎？

May I have another embarkation card [2]?

我可以再要一張旅客入境記錄卡嗎？

Could you tell me how to fill it in [3]?

你能告訴我怎麼填寫嗎？

How should I fill this in?

我要怎麼填寫這張表格？

Could you show me what to write here?

你能告訴我這裡要填什麼嗎？

Fill in this blank [4] with my address?

在這個填寫我的地址嗎？

I need that, too.

我也需要那個。

Phrase List

★**another** 另一個的

That's another matter.

那是另外一回事。

★**fill in** 填寫

You can fill in the blanks with your name.

在空格裡填上你的名字。

Word Bank

1. **declaration** *n.* 申報
2. **embarkation card** 入境記錄卡
3. **fill in** 填寫
4. **blank** *n.* 空白表格

EUROPE
AMERICA
ASIA
AFRICA
AUSTRALIA

Chapter 4

旅館住宿

MP3 038

Lesson 1

詢問空房

Do you have a twin room?

你們有兩張單人床的房間嗎？

I plan to stay here for 4 nights.

我計劃要在這裡住四晚。

OK. I will take it.

好，我要訂。

通常你會聽到對方這麼說：

◆We have an available.

我們目前有房。

I'd like a room for one.

我要一間單人房。

I'd like a room for two with separate beds.

我要一間有兩張床的房間。

Could you recommend another hotel?

你可以推薦另一個飯店嗎？

通常你會聽到對方這麼說：

◆I am sorry, sir, but we are all booked up.

抱歉，先生，我們全部客滿了。

Phrase List

★**for**+數字+可數名詞　為期一段時間

I'm planning to stay here for 2 days.

我正計劃要在這裡停留兩天。

★**recommend+sbdy.**+名詞　推薦某物給某人

Can you recommend me some new books?

你可以推薦一些新書給我嗎？

★**book up**　事先預約

The hotel is fully booked up this year.

今年旅館全部客滿了。

MP3 039

Lesson 2

詢問房價

How much per night?

(住宿)一晚要多少錢？

How much will it be?

要多少錢？

How much should I pay for a week?

一個星期得付多少錢？

Do you have any cheaper [1] rooms?

你們有任何便宜一點的房間嗎？

How much for a single room [2]?

單人房多少錢？

Are meals included [3]?

有包括餐點嗎？

Does the room rate [4] include breakfast?

住宿費有包括早餐嗎？

Phrase List

★**per**+名詞　每一個

These apples cost ten dollars per pound.

這些蘋果每磅十元。

The lunch is $250 per person.

午餐費是每人兩百五十元。

Phrase List

Word Bank

1. **cheaper**　*a.*　較便宜的
2. **single room** 單人房
3. **included**　*a.*　被包括的
4. **room rate** 房價

Word Bank

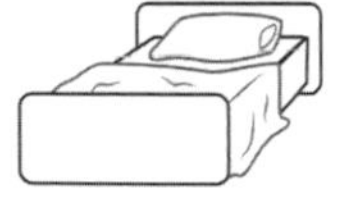

MP3 040

登記住宿

I would like to check in.

我要登記住宿。

Yes, I have a reservation[1]. My name is Tom Jones.

有的，我有預約訂房。我的名字是湯姆・瓊斯。

通常你會聽到對方這麼說：

◆Did you make a reservation?

您有預約住宿嗎？

I have a reservation for 2 nights.

我已訂了兩天住宿。

Here is the confirmation slip[2].

這是確認單。

I want a room with a sauna[3].

我想要有蒸汽浴的房間。

I want to stay for 4 more nights.

我想再多住四晚。

What's the floor[4]?

在幾樓？

Phrase List

★**make a reservation** 預約

I did make a reservation yesterday.

我昨天的確有預約。

★**on the+序號 floor** 在第…層樓

Our office is on the second floor.

我們辦公室在二樓。

Phrase List

Word Bank

1. **reservation** *n.* 預訂
2. **confirmation slip** 確認單
3. **sauna** *n.* 蒸汽浴
4. **floor** *n.* (樓房的)層

Word Bank

Lesson 4

飯店用餐

I forgot to bring my coupons [1] with me.

我忘了帶餐券。

Can I make a reservation for dinner?

我可以預約晚餐訂位嗎？

What time is breakfast served?

早餐什麼時候供應？

Where should I go to for the breakfast?

我應該去哪用餐？

I would like a table by the window.

我要靠窗戶的座位。

I want to reserve a table [2] for dinner tonight.

我想預訂今天的晚餐。

Please charge [3] it to my room. It's Room 714.

請將帳算在我的房間費用上，房間號碼是七一四。

Phrase List

Phrase List

★**forget to+**原形動詞　忘記去做某事

I forget to do my homework.

我忘了做我的功課。

★**reserve a table/seat**　預定餐桌/座位

I'd like to reserve 4 seats.

我想預訂四個座位。

Word Bank

1. **coupon** *n.* 配給券
2. **reserve a table** 預定座位
3. **charge** *v.* 要價

MP3 042

Lesson 5

表明身分

I am Jack Smith of Room 618.

我是618號房的傑克・史密斯

This is Room 916.

這是916號房。

My room number[1] is 316.

我的房間號碼是316。

Room 756. Key, please.

房號756。請給我鑰匙。

Phrase List

★I am+名字我是…名字

I am David Jones.

我是大衛・瓊斯。

★I am+身分 我是…身分

I am a student.

我是一位學生。

Word Bank

1. **room number** 房號

Word Bank

MP3 043

Lesson 6 客房服務

Give me a wake-up call[1] at eight, please.
請在八點打電話叫醒我。

I'd like a wake-up call every morning.
我每一天都要早上叫醒(的服務)。

I'd like an extra pillow[2] for Room 504.
我要在504房多加一個枕頭。

Would you bring us a bottle of[3] champagne?
你能帶一瓶香檳給我們嗎？

Let's see, and I want a chicken sandwich.
我想想，還有我要一份雞肉三明治。

I can't find any towels in my room.
我的房裡沒有毛巾。

Could you bring some towels right now[4]?

請你馬上送幾條毛巾過來好嗎？

The dryer doesn't work.

吹風機壞了。

Phrase List

★**right now** 現在、馬上

Where are you right now?

你現在在哪裡？

★**work** 運轉、作用

Does the machine work well?

這個機器運轉順利嗎？

Word Bank

1. **wake-up call** 早晨叫醒服務
2. **pillow** *n.* 枕頭
3. **a bottle of…** 一瓶…
4. **right now** 馬上

044

Lesson 7

衣物送洗

Do you have laundry service[1]?

你們有洗衣服務嗎？

I have some laundry[2].

我有一些衣服要送洗。

I'd like to send my suit to the cleaners[3].

我要把我的西裝送洗。

通常你會聽到對方這麼說：

◆Please put it in the plastic bag and leave it on the bed.

請放在塑膠袋裡，然後放在床上。

When can I have them returned?

我什麼時候可以拿回來？

I haven't gotten the coat back that I sent to the cleaners yesterday morning.

我昨天早上送洗的外套還沒送回來。

From what time do you accept[4] the laundry?
你們從什麼時候起受理送洗的衣物？

Phrase List

★**laundry** 送洗衣物

There's a lot of laundry in the basket.

籃子裡有很多要送洗的衣物。

★**send sthg. to** 將某物送至

I'd like to send the mail to my parents.

我要寄這封信給我的父母。

Word Bank

1. **laundry service** 洗衣服務
2. **laundry** *n.* 送洗的衣服
3. **cleaners** *n.* 乾洗店
4. **accept** *v.* 接受、領受

MP3 045

Lesson 8

旅館設施

There is no hot water in my room.
我的房間裡沒有熱水。

There is something wrong with the toilet.
廁所有點問題。

The lock of my room is broken.
我房間的鎖壞了。

The toilet in my room doesn't work properly[1].
我房間的廁所壞了。

I think the filament has broken.
我想燈絲壞了。

The water doesn't drain[2].
水流不出來。

My phone is out of order[3].
我的電話故障了。

Is there a beauty salon in the hotel?
旅館中有美容院嗎？

Phrase List

★**something wrong with** 某物有問題

There is something wrong with this room.

這個房間有點問題。

★**be broken** 損壞

My dryer is broken.

我的吹風機壞了。

★**out of order** 發生故障

The elevator is out of order.

電梯故障了。

Word Bank

1. **properly** **ad***v.* 正確地
2. **drain** *v.* 使流出
3. **out of order** 故障

MP3 046

Lesson 9 退房

Check out [1], please.
請結帳。

When is check-out time [2]?
退房的時間是什麼時候？

I would like to check out.
我要結帳。

Here is the room key.
這是房間鑰匙。

Phrase List

★**check out** 結帳、退房

When can I check out?
我什麼時候可以退房？

Can I check out later?
我可以稍後再結帳嗎？

Word Bank

1. **check out** 退房
2. **check-out time** 退房的時間

MP3 047

Lesson 10

結帳

How much does it charge?
這要收多少錢？

Put it on my hotel bill [1], please.
請算在我的住宿費裡。

Can I pay with a traveler's check?
我可以用旅行支票付嗎？

I will pay cash [2].
我會付現金。

通常你會聽到對方這麼說：

◆How would you like to pay it, sir?
先生，您要怎麼付錢呢？

I am afraid there is something wrong with the bill.
帳單恐怕有點問題。

Are the service charges and tax included?
是否包括服務費和稅金嗎？

Are there any additional[3] charges?
是否有其他附加費用？

Phrase List

★**charge** 收費
The store doesn't charge for delivery.
該商店免費送貨。

★**pay cash** 用現金支付
Will you pay cash?
你會用現金支付嗎？

Word Bank

1. bill *n.* 帳單
2. cash *n.* 現金、現款
3. additional *a.* 附加的、額外的

Phrase List
Word Bank

MP3 048

Lesson 11

一般飯店常用語

Don't disturb [1].

請勿打擾。（房間標語）

Who is it, please?

是誰？

I'd like to change my room.

我想換房間。

Where can I find the tourist information counter [2]?

請問旅客服務台在哪裡？

Do I have any messages [3]?

我有任何的留言嗎？

This is Mary Jones in Room 602. Do you have any messages for me?

我是602室的瑪莉・瓊斯。有沒有給我的留言？

If someone comes to see me, please give him this message.
如果有人來找我，請將這留言交給他。

Do I have to leave the room key when I go out?
在我外出時必須要留下房間鑰匙嗎？

I have lost my room key.
我遺失了我的房間鑰匙了。

I left my key in my room.
我把我的房間鑰匙放在房間裡（忘了帶出來）。

I locked myself out [4].
我把自己反鎖在外面。

Where is the locker [5]?
寄物櫃在哪裡？

Could you keep my baggage till two o'clock?
請你幫我保管行李到兩點鐘好嗎？

I'd like to pick up my baggage.
我要拿我的行李。

Will you keep these valuables [6] for me?
請幫我保管這些貴重物品好嗎？

Key to Room 306, please.

(我要拿)房號306的鑰匙。

My room number is 306.

我的房間號碼是306。

Could you call me a taxi, please? I'm going to the airport.

請你幫我叫部計程車好嗎？我要去機場。

Is this coin [7] all right for telephones?

這個硬幣可以打電話嗎？

Could you connect [8] me with the telephone directory assistance [9]?

可以幫我接查號台嗎？

How do I call a number outside this hotel?

我要怎麼從飯店撥外線出去？

通常你會聽到對方這麼說：

◆Dial 9 first, and then the phone number.

先撥九，再撥電話號碼。

Word Bank

1. **disturb** *v.* 妨礙、打擾
2. **tourist information counter** 旅客服務台
3. **message** *n.* 口信、信息、消息
4. **lock myself out** 將自己反鎖
5. **locker** *n.* 衣物櫃
6. **valuable** *n.* 貴重物品
7. **coin** *n.* 硬幣
8. **connect** *v.* 給...接通電話
9. **telephone directory assistance** 查號台

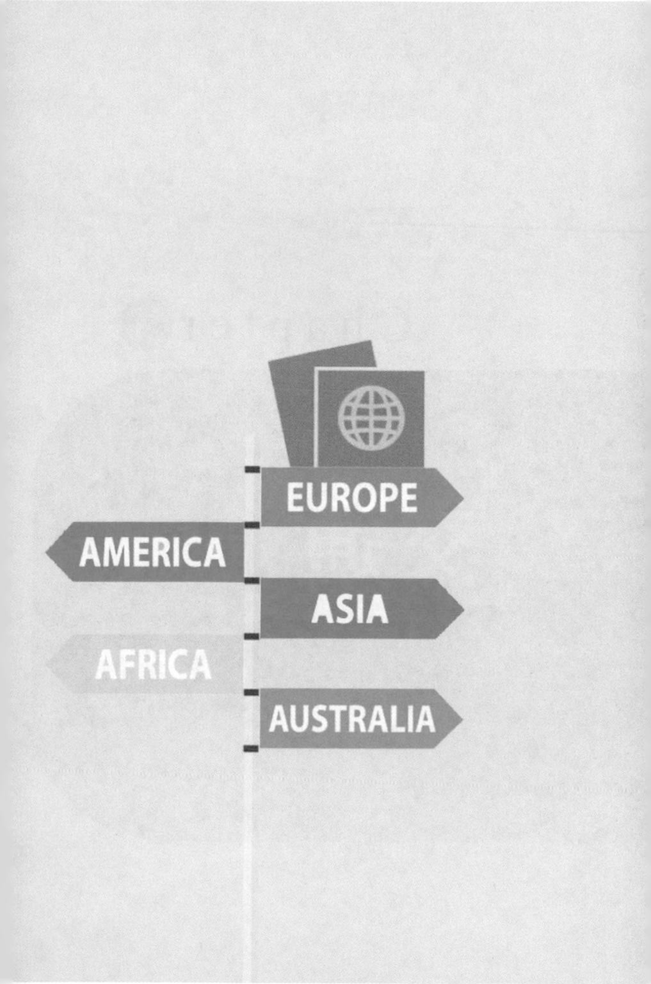

EUROPE
AMERICA
ASIA
AFRICA
AUSTRALIA

EUROPE
AMERICA
ASIA
AFRICA
AUSTRALIA

Chapter 5

交通

MP3 049

Lesson 1

前往會場

I'll meet you at the airport.
我會去機場接你。

Can I get there on foot [1]?
我可以用走的到那裡嗎？

Where is the TICC?
台北國際會議中心在哪裡？

I have to be there by 9 o'clock.
我要在九點前到那裡。

Can you tell me how to get there?
你能告訴我怎麼到那裡嗎？

Do you have the map of the downtown?
你有市中心的地圖嗎？

Is there any transportation [2] to get there?
有大眾運輸系統到那裡嗎？

Do you know the address of TICC?
你知道台北國際會議中心的地址嗎？

Phrase List

★**meet sbdy. at the airport** 到機場接機

I'll meet her at the airport.

我會去機場接她的飛機。

★**on foot** 用步行

Maybe we should get there on foot.

也許我們可以用走的到那裡。

★**by+時間** 在某個時間點之前

I'll be there by two pm.

我要在下午兩點前到達那裡。

Word Bank

1. on foot 用走路的方式

2. transportation *n.* 運輸工具

050

Lesson 2

時間、路程

How long will it take?

需要多久的時間？

How long will it take to get there?

到那兒要花多長的時間？

How long will it take to get to your office?

到你的辦公室要多久的時間？

I will be there on time.

我會準時到達。

Can you get me to there in twenty minutes?

你可以在二十分鐘內送我到達嗎？

How far from here?

從這裏去有多遠？

通常你會聽到對方這麼說：

◆It is about 5 miles.

大約有五哩。

◆It takes just five minute's walk.

走路只需要五分鐘。

Phrase List

★**in+**時間　在某個時間點之內

I'll be there in 10 minutes.

我會在十分鐘內到達。

Would you be there in twenty minutes?

你會在廿分鐘內到達那裡嗎？

★數字+**minute's walk**　...分鐘的步行

It'll take 10 minute's walk.

走路會需要十分鐘。

It'll take you five minute's walk.

它要花你走路五分鐘的時間。

051

Lesson 3

迷路

Excuse me, can you do me favor?

抱歉，你能幫我一個忙嗎？

I am lost [1].

我迷路了。

Do you know where the Museum is?

你知道博物館在哪裡嗎？

Can I get some directions [2]?

能問一下路嗎？

Can you direct [3] me to the police office?

你能告訴我去警察局怎麼走嗎？

Would you tell me how to go to the Railway Station?

你能告訴我如何去火車站嗎？

Where can I take a taxi [4]?

我可以在哪裡搭乘計程車？

Phrase List

★**lost** 迷路、迷惘

I am lost.

我迷路了。

I get lost.

我搞混了。

★**take a taxi** 搭乘計程車

You may take a taxi.

你可以搭乘計程車。

Phrase List

Word Bank

1. **be lost** 迷路
2. **direction** *n.* 方向、方位
3. **direct** *v.* 指引方向
4. **take a taxi** 搭乘計程車

Word Bank

MP3 052

Lesson 4
交通意外

I was tied up in traffic [1].
我遇到塞車。

My car broke down.
我的車子壞了。

The tire blew [2] out.
車胎爆了。

My car broke down on the freeway.
我的車在高速公路上拋錨了。

The fire burnt out.
火熄滅了。

The engine is burnt out.
引擎燒壞了。

The train was behind time [3].
火車晚點了。

Can you lend me a pump to blow up my tires?
你能借給我打氣筒給輪胎打氣嗎？

Phrase List

★**be tied up** 受困

I was tied up at the moment.

我現在很忙。

★**blow sthg. out** 中止

I blow the candle out.

我吹熄蠟燭。

★**burn sthg. out** 熄滅

The small fire can be left to burn itself out.

這場小火不必理會就會自行熄滅。

Word Bank

1. **tied up in traffic** 困在車陣中
2. **blow** *v.* 吹
3. **behind time** 延遲

Lesson 5 火車、地鐵、捷運

Where can I buy the ticket?
我要去哪裡買車票？

A one-way/round-trip ticket to New York, please.
一張到紐約的單程/來回票。

Which train goes to New York?
哪一班車廂到紐約？

Is this the right line for New York?
去紐約是這條路線嗎？

Is this the right platform [1] for New York?
這是出發到紐約的月台嗎？

Where should I transfer to New York?
我要到哪裡轉車到紐約？

Where should I change trains for New York?
去紐約要去哪裡換車？

Where should I get off [2] to go to New York?

到紐約要在哪裡下車？

Phrase List

★**get off** 下車

When should I get off?

我什麼時候應該要下車？

Word Bank

1. **platform** *n.* (鐵路、捷運等的)月台
2. **get off** 下車

MP3 054

Lesson 6
公車

Does this bus go to New York?
這部公車有到紐約嗎？

Is this bus stop for New York?
這個站牌有到紐約嗎？

Does this bus stop at City Hall?
這公車在市政府站有停嗎？

What is the fare [1]?
車資是多少？

How often does this bus run [2]?
公車多久來一班？

How many stops are there to Taipei?
到台北有多少個站？

Would you please tell me when we get there?
我們到達時可否告訴我一聲？

Let me off here, please.
我要在這裡下車。

Phrase List

★**how often+**助動詞 多經常做某事

How often do you call your parents?

你多久打電話給你的父母？

Word Bank

1. fare *n.* (交通工具的)票價

2. run *v.* (車、船)行駛

MP3 055

Lesson 7

計程車

Please take me to this address.

請載我到這個地址。

Can I get there by five o'clock?

我五點前到得了那裡嗎？

City Hall, please.

請到市政府。

Could you drive faster?

你能開快一點嗎？

Turn right at the first corner.

在第一個轉彎處右轉。

Let me off at the traffic light.

讓我在紅綠燈處下車。

How much is the fare?

車資是多少？

通常你會聽到對方這麼說：

◆It's two hundred and fifty dollars.

總共二百五十元。

Keep the change.
不用找零。

Phrase List

★**take sbdy. to** 帶某人至某處

Did you take her to the hospital?

你帶她去醫院了嗎？

Would you take me to the hospital?

可以請你送我到醫院嗎？

★**turn right/left** 右/左轉

Turn right and you'll see it.

右轉你就會看到。

You can turn left at the corner.

你可以在轉角左轉。

Phrase List

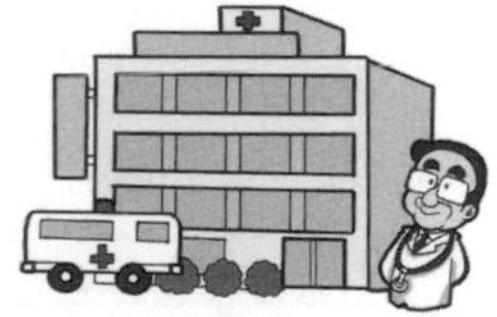

MP3 056

Lesson 8

租車

I would like to rent a car.
我要租車。

I would like a Toyota.
我要（租）豐田的車。

I will need it from this Monday to Friday.
我這個星期一到星期五需要這部車。

I would like to reserve one car for a week.
我要預約一個星期的車。

What's the rate for a wagon?
租一輛客貨兩用車要多少錢？

How much does it cost to rent a car?
租用一輛車需要多少錢？

通常你會聽到對方這麼說：

◆The daily rate is 1,500 dollars.
每天的租金是一千五百元。

Do I have to return the car here?

我要回到這裡還車嗎？

I will take it right now.

我現在就要。

Phrase List

★**rent a car** 租車

I'd like to rent a car tomorrow.

我明天要租車。

★**take it** 選購、決定要

Can I take it right now?

我可以現在就要嗎？

EUROPE
AMERICA
ASIA
AFRICA
AUSTRALIA

EUROPE
AMERICA
ASIA
AFRICA
AUSTRALIA

Chapter 6

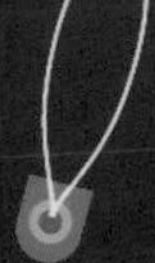

電話聯絡

MP3 057

Lesson 1 去電找人

Is Chris around [1]?
克里斯在嗎？

Is Annie in today?
安妮今天在嗎？

Is Brian in the office now?
布萊恩現在在辦公室裡嗎？

Hello, may I speak to Dr. Brown?
哈囉，我能和布朗教授說話嗎？

May I speak to Chris, please?
我能和克里斯說話嗎？

Could I talk to Carrie or Sunny?
我能和凱莉或桑尼說話嗎？

This is Luke calling for [2] Miss Simon.
我是路克打電話來要找賽門小姐。

Is this Mrs. White?
您是懷特太太嗎？

Phrase List

★**be around** 在附近

Is Mr. White around?

懷特先生在嗎？

★**speak to sbdy.** 和某人說話

I'd like to speak to John.

我要和約翰說話。

Phrase List

Word Bank

1. around *adv.* 附近

2. call for 來電尋找（某人）

Word Bank

Lesson 2

詢問受話方現況

Is Sophia off the line?
蘇菲亞講完電話了嗎？

Where is he?
他人在哪裡？

May I have his phone number?
可以給我他的電話號碼嗎？

Do you know when he would come back?
你知道他什麼時候會回來嗎？

When will he come back?
他什麼時候會回來？

Do you know when he will be back?
你知道他什麼時候會回來？

Do you know where I can reach [1] him?
你知道我在哪裡可以聯絡上他嗎？

Do you have any idea [2] where he is now?
你知道他現在在哪裡嗎？

Phrase List

★be off the line 講完電話

Is he off the line?

他講完電話了嗎？

★come back 回來

I'll come back tomorrow night.

我明天晚上會回來。

★reach sbdy. 聯絡上某人

I didn't know how to reach him.

我不知道要如何聯絡上他。

Phrase List

Word Bank

1. reach sbdy. 聯絡某人

2. have any idea 是否知道

Word Bank

MP3 059

Lesson 3
回電

I am returning your call[1].
我現在回你電話。

You called me last night, didn't you?
你昨天打電話給我，不是嗎？

Thank you for returning my call.
謝謝你回我電話。

That's all right. I will try to call him later.
沒關係。我晚一點再打電話給他。

I will try again later.
我晚一點再試一次（打電話）。

When should I call back[2] then?
那我應該什麼時候回電？

Can I call again in 10 minutes?
我可以十分鐘後再打電話過來嗎？

Would you tell him I called?
你能告訴他我來電過嗎？

Phrase List

★**return sbdy's call** 回某人電話

I'll return her call.

我會回她的電話。

★**thank you for**+動名詞 感謝你做了某事

Thank you for coming back.

感謝你趕回來。

★**call back** 回電

I should call back later.

我應該稍後回電。

Word Bank

1. return someone's call 回某人電話

2. call back 回電

MP3 060

Lesson 4

本人接電話

Speaking.
請說。

This is Kate Simon.
我是凱特・賽門。

This is he/she.
我就是你要找的人

It's me.
我就是。

I can't talk to you now.
我現在不能講（電話）。

I am really busy now. I will call you later.
我現在真的很忙。我待會打電話給你。

Who is calling, please?
您是哪一位？

Would you mind [1] calling back later?
你介意等一下再打電話過來嗎？

Phrase List

★**talk to sbdy.** 和某人講話/通電話

I'm not allowed to talk to you.

我不允許和你通電話。

★**mind+**動名詞　介意做某事

I do mind coming again.

我會介意要再來一次。

Phrase List

Word Bank

1. mind *v.* 介意、反對

Word Bank

MP3 061

Lesson 5 代接電話

I am sorry, but he is busy with another line[1].
很抱歉，他正在忙線中。

Wait a moment, please. I will get him.
請稍等，我去叫他。

Let me see if hc is in.
我看看他在不在。

You can try again in a few minutes[2].
你可以過幾分鐘再打來看看。

Which Tom do you want to talk to?
你要和哪一個湯姆說話？

Do you know his extension[3]?
你知道他的分機嗎？

Phrase List

★**be busy with another line** 忙線中

Is he is busy with another line?

他正在忙線中嗎？

★**let sbdy.+**原型動詞 讓某人做某事

Let him make the decision.

就讓他做決定。

Phrase List

Word Bank

1. **be busy with another line** 忙線中
2. **in a few minutes** 再過幾分鐘
3. **extension** *n.* 分機

Word Bank

MP3 062

Lesson 6

無法接電話

Mr. Jones is on another line [1].
瓊斯先生正忙線中。

He is busy with another line.
他正在另一條線上（講電話）。

I am sorry, but he is in a meeting [2] now.
很抱歉，他現在正在開會中。

He will be back after 2 o'clock.
他會在兩點之後回來。

He is busy at present [3] and can't speak to you.
他現在很忙，不能跟你說話。

I am sorry, but he is not at his desk [4] now.
很抱歉，他現在不在座位上。

I am sorry, but he just went out.
很抱歉，他剛出去。

I am afraid he is not here.
他恐怕不在這裡。

Phrase List

★in a meeting 開會中

Is he still in a meeting now?

他現在還在開會中嗎？

★at present 目前

I don't need the bill at present.

我現在不需要帳單。

Word Bank

1. **be on another line** 在另一線電話通話中
2. **meeting** *n.* 會議
3. **at present** 目前
4. **be at sbdy's desk** 在某人的座位上

MP3 063

轉接電話

I will put you through[1].
我幫你接過去。

I will transfer your call[2].
我幫你轉接電話。

I'll connect you.
我幫你轉接電話。

I'm connecting you now.
我現在就幫你轉接電話過去。

Could you put me through to John Martin, ple-ase?
能幫我轉接電話給約翰・馬丁嗎？

Would you tell her to answer[3] my call first? This is urgent.
可以請你轉告她先接我的電話嗎？這是急事。

I will connect you to extension 747.
我幫你轉到分機747。

I will transfer your call to the marketing department.

我會幫你轉接到行銷部門。

Phrase List

Phrase List

★**put sbdy. through** 轉接某人電話

I'll put you through.

我會幫你把電話轉接過去。

★**transfer someone's call** 轉接某人電話

I'll transfer her call.

我會把她的電話轉接過去。

★**connect sbdy.** 給某人接通電話

I'll connect you.

我幫你轉接電話。

Word Bank

Word Bank

1. **put through** 轉接
2. **transfer call** 轉接電話
3. **answer** *v.* 回答、答覆

MP3 064

Lesson 8

詢問來電者身分

Who is this?
您是哪位？

May I ask who is calling?
請問您是哪位？

May I know who is calling?
請問您的大名？

Who is calling, please?
請問您的大名？

Who should I say is calling?
我要說是誰來電？

May I have your name, please?
請問您的大名？

Are you Mr. Jones?
您是瓊斯先生嗎？

You are...?
您是…？

Phrase List

★**who be**動詞+動名詞　誰正在做某事

Who is walking on the street?

誰在街道上行走？

★**May I**+原型動詞　我能否…

May I have your name?

請問您的大名？

Phrase List

MP3 065

Lesson 9

電話約定會面

Let me see my schedule[1]. When do you prefer[2]?
我看看我的行程。你想要什麼時候？

How about ten o'clock tomorrow morning?
明天早上十點如何？

Mary, can you come to a meeting on Friday?
瑪莉，妳星期五能參加會議嗎？

Let me check my schedule and call you back.
讓我查查我的行程再回你電話。

We're planning on having it around noon [3].
我們計劃在中午舉行(會議)。

If I'm not in, could you leave a message on my answering machine [4]?
如果我不在，你能留言在我的答錄機嗎？

I will tell him to be on time.
我會告訴他要準時。

Phrase List

★**how about**+名詞　某人/事/物如何

How about Tom? He is the best one.

湯姆如何？他是最棒的人選。

★**leave a message**　留下訊息

Would you like to leave a message?

您要留言嗎？

Word Bank

1. **schedule** *n.* 行程
2. **prefer** *v.* 偏好
3. **noon** *n.* 中午
4. **answering machine** 答錄機

MP3 066

Lesson 10

電話留言

Could I leave him a message [1]?
我能留言給他嗎？

May I take a message?
需要我(替你)留言嗎？

Would you tell Mr. Jones David called, please?
能請您告訴瓊斯先生，大衛打過電話嗎？

Tell her to give me a call as soon as possible [2].
告訴她盡快回我電話。

Sure, my number is 8547-3663.
好的，我的號碼是8547-3663。

Would you ask him to call Mark at 8547-3663?
你能請他打電話到8547-3663給馬克嗎？

Call me at 5697-1000, extension 27, after ten.
十點以後，打電話到 5697-1000 分機 27 給我。

I will have [3] him call you back.
我會請他回你電話。

Phrase List

★**leave sbdy. a message** 留訊息給某人

You can leave him a message.

您可以留言給他。

★**as soon as possible** 盡快

You need to go home as soon as possible.

你應該要盡快回家。

★**have sbdy.**+原形動詞 要求某人做某事

I'll have her change her mind.

我會讓她改變她的想法。

Word Bank

1. **message** *n.* 口信、信息、消息
2. **as soon as possible** 盡快
3. **have** *v.* 要求

MP3 067

Lesson 11 打錯電話

I'm afraid you've got the wrong number.
你恐怕撥錯電話了。

You must have the wrong number.
你一定是打錯號碼了。

What number are you dialing [1]?
你打幾號？

I am calling 6987-2201.
我撥的電話是6987-2201。

Is this 8647-3663?
這是8647-3663嗎？

I am sorry, but there is no one here by that name.
很抱歉，這裡沒有這個人。

There is no David here.
這裡沒有大衛這個人。

Phrase List

★**have the wrong number** 撥錯電話

Did I have the wrong number?

我打錯電話號碼了嗎？

★**dial number** 撥電話號碼

You must dial the wrong number.

你一定撥錯電話號碼了。

Phrase List

Word Bank

1. dial *v.* 撥(電話號碼)

Word Bank

068

Lesson 12 結束通話

I've got to hang up[1] the phone.
我要掛電話了。

I have to get going.
我要掛電話了。

I'd better get off the phone[2].
我必須掛電話了。

I've got to leave now.
我要走了。

Nice talking to you.
很高興和你說話。

Thank you for calling.
謝謝你打電話來。

You can call me anytime[3].
歡迎隨時打電話給我。

Just give me a call when you have a chance[4].
有空要打電話給我。

Phrase List

★**hang up** 掛斷電話

Don't hang up the phone.

不要掛電話。

★**get off the phone** 掛斷電話

We'll leave home when he gets off the phone.

他掛斷電話後，我們就要出門了。

★**have a chance** 有機會

We have a chance to work in the USA.

我們有機會在美國工作。

Word Bank

1. **hang up** 掛斷電話
2. **get off the phone** 結束通話
3. **anytime** *adv.* 在任何時候
4. **have a chance** 有機會、有時間

MP3 069

Lesson 13

電話中的疑問

I'm sorry, but I don't understand.
抱歉，我不懂。

Could you repeat [1] that, please?
能請你再說一遍嗎？

Pardon [2]?
你說什麼？

I can't hear you very well.
我聽不清楚你說什麼。

Could you speak up [3] a little, please?
能請你說大聲一點嗎？

Your line is always engaged [4].
你的電話一直佔線中。

Could you spell your name, please?
能請你拼一遍你的名字嗎？

Does he have your number?
他知道你的號碼嗎？

Phrase List

★**hear sbdy.** 聽見某人

What did you say? I can't hear you.

你說什麼？我聽不見你(說什麼)。

★**speak up** 大聲地

You have to speak up.

你必須要說大聲一點。

★**be engaged** 被佔用的

The number is engaged.

電話正在佔線中。

Word Bank

1. repeat *v.* 重說

2. pardon *n.* 原諒（請再說一遍）

3. speak up 大聲説

4. engaged *a.* 忙於

MP3 070

Lesson 14

電話常用短語

Hello?
哈囉？

I hope I didn't disturb you.
我希望我沒有打擾你。

I am sorry to call you so late.
我很抱歉這麼晚打電話給你。

Am I calling at a bad time?
我打來得不是時候嗎？

Hi, Barry. Got a minute [1] now?
嗨，貝瑞，現在有空嗎？

Hold on, please.
請稍等。

Just a minute, please.
請等一下。

Would you wait a moment, please?
能請你稍等一下嗎？

Could you hold the line [2], please?
能請你稍等不要掛斷電話嗎？

Hold the line, please.
請稍等不要掛斷電話。

Can you hold?
您要等嗎？

Keep going.
説吧！

Thank you for waiting.
謝謝你等這麼久。

Sorry to have kept you waiting.
抱歉讓你久等了。

My call did not go through [3].
我的電話並沒有撥通。

I was just about to call you.
我剛好要打電話給您。

Please give me the phone number of Mr. Kim.
請給我金先生的電話號碼。

Phrase List

★**disturb sbdy.** 打擾某人

Did I disturb you?

我有打擾你嗎？

★**hold on** 不掛斷電話

Hold on a second, please.

請稍等一下。

★**hold the line** 不掛斷電話

Would you hold the line, please?

請您稍等不要掛斷電話。

★**keep+**動名詞 持續不斷做某事

They keep asking me questions.

他們一直問我問題。

Phrase List

Word Bank

1. **got a minute** 有空閒時間
2. **hold the line** 不要掛斷電話
3. **go through** （電話）撥通

Word Bank

EUROPE
AMERICA
ASIA
AFRICA
AUSTRALIA

EUROPE
AMERICA
ASIA
AFRICA
AUSTRALIA

Chapter 7

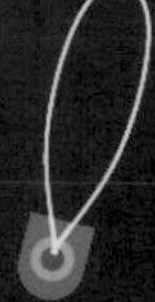

拜訪客戶

MP3 071

Lesson 1

拜訪客戶

Is Mr. Robinson in?
羅賓森先生在嗎？

May I see Mr. Robinson?
我可以見羅賓森先生嗎？

I would like to see Mr. Robinson.
我要見羅賓森先生。

你也可以這麼說：
◆I would like to meet Mr. Robinson.
我要見羅賓森先生。

I am here to see Mr. Robinson.
我來這裡見羅賓森先生。

Hello, Mrs. Jones. Can I see Mr. Robinson now?
哈囉！瓊斯女士。我現在能見羅賓森先生嗎？

Phrase List

Phrase List

★**be here to**+原形動詞　在此地做某事

I am here to meet my friend Joseph.

我來這裡和我的朋友約瑟夫見面。

She is here to figure it out.

她來這裡查清楚。

We are here to solve this problem.

我們來這裡解決這個問題。

MP3 072

Lesson 2

與客戶有約

I have an appointment[1] with Mr. Robinson.

我和羅賓森先生有約。

I have an appointment with Mr. Robinson for 3 o'clock.

我和羅賓森先生三點有約。

Yes, it's for 2 o'clock, but I am little early[2].

有的，我兩點有約，但是我提早到。

通常你會聽到對方這麼說：

◆Do you have an appointment?

您有事先約嗎？

Is Mr. Robinson ready to see me?

羅賓森先生準備要見我了嗎？

Sorry, I am late. Is Mr. Robinson still here?

對不起我遲到了。羅賓森先生還在這裡嗎？

Mr. Robinson invited me to meet him.

羅賓森先生邀請我來見他。

Phrase List

★**have an appointment** 有預約

Did you have an appointment?

你有預約嗎？

★**be ready to**+原形動詞 準備好要做某事

Are you ready to leave?

你準備要離開了嗎？

★**invite sbdy. to**+原形動詞 邀請某人做某事

They invited us to climb the hill.

他們約我們出去爬山。

Word Bank

1. **have an appointment** 有約定
2. **early** *adv.* 提早

MP3 073

Lesson 3 沒有事先預約

I don't have an appointment.
我沒有事先約。

No, I don't have an appointment.
沒有，我沒有事先約。

通常你會聽到對方這麼說：
◆Do you have an appointment?
您有事先約嗎？

May I make an appointment [1] with Mr. Robinson?
能安排我和羅賓森先生見面嗎？

Would you give me an hour to talk with Mr. Robinson?
我想跟羅賓森先生談談，只要一個小時就行。

What time is he available [2]?
他什麼時候有空？

Could you arrange a meeting with Mr. Jones for me?
能請你幫我安排和瓊斯先生的會面嗎？

Phrase List

★arrange a meeting 安排會面

I've got to arrange a meeting with you.

我必須要安排和你會面。

Word Bank

1. make an appointment 安排會面

2. available *a.* 有空的

MP3 074

Lesson 4
說明來訪目的

It's about a new contract[1].
是有關新合約的事。

He invited me to this meeting.
他邀請我參加會議。

We are supposed to[2] meet at five.
我們原本預計五點見面的。

I was wondering[3] if he is interested[4] in our products.
我是在想他是否對我們的商品有興趣？

Can you tell him I am here to discuss[5] sales promotions?
你能告訴他我是來這裡討論行銷計畫嗎？

We are here to attend the annual[6] meeting.
我們來這裡參加年度會議。

常你會聽到對方這麼說：
◆Why do you wish to see him?
您為什麼要見他？

Phrase List

★**be supposed to+**原形動詞

I'm supposed to take a taxi.

我原本應該要搭計程車。

★**be interested in** 對...有興趣

I'm interested in your projects.

我對你們的企畫案有興趣。

Phrase List

Word Bank

1. **contract** *n.* 合約
2. **be supposed to** 原訂要…
3. **wondering** *a.* 疑惑的
4. **be interested in...** 對…有興趣
5. **discuss** *v.* 討論
6. **annual** *a.* 年度的

Word Bank

Lesson 5

自我介紹

Hi, I am Sophia Jones from Taiwan.
嗨，我是來自台灣的蘇菲亞・瓊斯。

I came from London.
我來自倫敦。

David White of BCQ Company.
(我是) BCQ的大衛・懷特。

Sophia Jones. I called on [1] Mr. Lee yesterday.
(我是)蘇菲亞・瓊斯。昨天我拜訪過李先生。

I am Sophia Jones, and this is my co-worker [2] David White.
我是蘇菲亞・瓊斯，這位是我同事大衛・懷特。

I am Sophia Jones.
我是蘇菲亞・瓊斯。

通常你會聽到對方這麼說：

◆May I have your name, please?

請問您的大名？

Phrase List

★**call on sbdy.** 拜訪某人

I'll call on you this Saturday.

我這個週六會去拜訪你。

Word Bank

1. **call on** 拜訪
2. **co-worker** 同事

MP3 076

Lesson 6 問候客戶

Hello, David, how are you?
哈囉，大衛，你好嗎？

It's nice to meet you, Mr. Jones.
瓊斯先生，很高興與你見面。

How is your business?
生意好嗎？

How have you been?
近來好嗎？

How were your weeks?
這星期過得如何？

How is your family?
你的家人好嗎？

Please say hello to Kathy for me.
幫我向凱西問候。

What are you working on?
你在忙些什麼？

Phrase List

★**work on + sthg.** 致力於某事

I've worked on this project for 3 months.

我已經忙這個企劃案三個月了。

How long did you work on it?

這件事你忙多久了？

MP3 077

Lesson 7 客套用語

Thank you for inviting me.

感謝你邀請我。

Thank you for your time.

感謝您的撥冗。

You look busy.

你看起來好像很忙！

It's been a long time.

好久不見。

I'm happy to meet you.
很高興見到你。

It's nice meeting you.
很高興認識你。

I'm glad to see you again.
很高興再次見到你。

It's nice meeting you, too.
我也很高興認識你。

It's my honor to see you.
能見到你是我的榮幸。

Phrase List

★sbdy. look+形容詞　某人看起來...

You look upset.

你看起很沮喪！

★a long time　很長一段時間

I've not seen you for a long time.

好久沒見到你。

Phrase List

078

Lesson 8

洽談公事

I need to talk with you about our plans.
我需要和您談談我們的計畫。

How would you like to solve this problem [1]?
您要如何解決這個問題？

I think we will take the responsibility [2].
我覺得我們會負責。

We hope you will consider [3] our proposal.
我們希望你能考慮我們的提案。

It's a great offer [4], isn't it?
這是一個很好的提案，不是嗎？

Do you mind if we make some suggestions [5]?
您介意我們提一些建議嗎？

We need to talk about the details [6].
我們需要討論有關細節的事。

We are offering a special plan.
我們提供一份促銷的提議。

Phrase List

★**solve the problem** 解決問題

I've no idea how to solve this problem.

我不知道要如何解決這個問題。

★**take the responsibility** 負責任

I'll take the responsibility.

我會負責任。

Phrase List

Word Bank

1. **solve this problem** 解決這個問題
2. **responsibility** *n.* 責任
3. **consider** *v.* 考慮
4. **offer** *v.* 提議
5. **suggestion** *n.* 建議
6. **detail** *n.* 細節

Word Bank

MP3 079

Lesson 9

熱絡氣氛

Have you ever been to Japan?
你去過日本嗎？

We are looking forward to [1] seeing you.
我們都很期待見到您。

I am looking forward to the next meeting.
我期待下一次的會議。

It's my pleasure to be one of your members [2].
我非常榮幸能成為你們的一員。

I am so happy to cooperate [3] with you.
我很高興與你合作。

May I come in on your plan?
我能參與你們的計畫嗎？

I will call on you tomorrow.
我明早會去拜訪你。

你也可以這麼說：

◆I shall call at you tomorrow.
我明天要到你家裏拜訪。

Phrase List

Phrase List

★**look forward to**+動名詞　期待做某事

I'm looking forward to seeing you.

我很期待見到您。

★**look forward to**+名詞　期待某事

I'm looking forward to the party.

我很期待這個宴會。

★**call at sbdy.** 到某人家裡拜訪

I'll call at you next Friday.

我下個星期五會去拜訪你。

Word Bank

Word Bank

1. **look forward to**　期待
2. **member**　*n.*　會員
3. **cooperate**　*v.*　合作

MP3 080

Lesson 10

建立友誼

Dinner is on me.
晚飯我請客。

Let's take a break.
我們休息一下。

I am willing to go with you.
我樂意和你去。

I will call for you tomorrow morning.
我明天早上去接你。

你也可以這麼說：
◆I'll come for you at 9 o'clock.
我九點來接你。

Let's go visit Mr. Robinson.
讓我們去拜訪羅賓森先生吧！

Give me a call when you arrive in Taiwan.
你到台灣時一定要打電話給我。

It's been lovely meeting you.
真是高興能夠和你們見面。

Phrase List

★take a break 休息片刻

You may take a break.

你們可以休息片刻。

★be willing to+原形動詞 極願意做某事

I'm willing to help you.

我非常樂意幫助你。

★call for sbdy. 接載某人

I'll call for you at five.

我五點去接你。

Phrase List

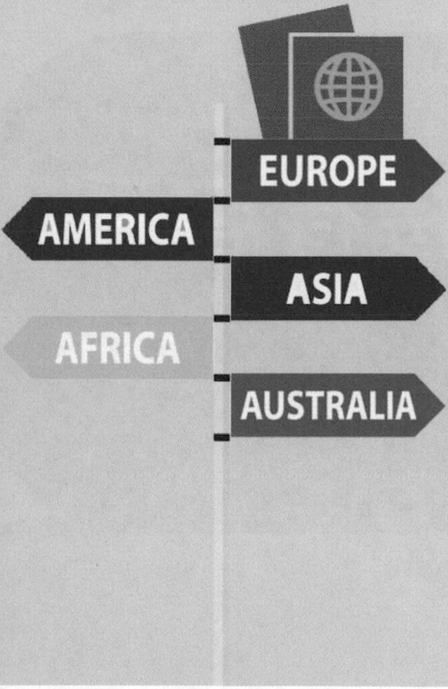

EUROPE

AMERICA

ASIA

AFRICA

AUSTRALIA

Chapter 8

接待客戶

MP3 081

Lesson 1

確認身分

Excuse me, are you Mr. Smith?
抱歉，請問你是史密斯先生嗎？

Are you Mr. Smith?
您是史密斯先生嗎？

Mr. Smith?
史密斯先生？

May I have your name, please?
請問您的大名？

Are you Mr. Smith of BCM?
您是BCM公司的史密斯先生嗎？

Mr. Smith? Here!
史密斯先生？在這裡！

I am David Jones of CNS Company.
我是CNS公司的大衛・瓊斯。

How do you do? I am Sophia Jones.
你好嗎？我是蘇菲亞・瓊斯。

Phrase List

★**excuse me** 抱歉我的打擾

Excuse me, may I see Mr. Smith now?

抱歉，我現在可以見史密斯先生嗎？

Excuse us. We've got to leave now.

抱歉。我們現在必須要離開。

★主句, **please?** 請...

Would you do me a favor, please?

可以請你幫我的忙嗎？

May I have your name, please?

請問您的大名？

MP3 082

Lesson 2

客套用語

Good morning/Good afternoon/Good evening.

早安／午安／晚安。

Welcome, Mr. Taylor.

泰勒先生，歡迎你！

Glad to meet you here.

很高興在這裡見到你。

I'm glad to meet you too.

我也非常高興與你見面。

How nice to see you again.

再次見到你很高興。

You haven't changed at all.

你一點都沒變。

Thank you for coming.

感謝你來。

Phrase List

★**how**+形容詞　多麼地…

How beautiful you are.

你真可愛。

How adorable she is.

她真是可愛。

★**at all**　完全地、終究

You haven't done anything well at all.

你什麼事都沒做好。

He is my only family after all.

終究他還是我唯一的家人。

MP3 083

Lesson 3

招待客戶

Just a minute, please.
請等一下。

Sit down please, Mr. Smith.
請坐，史密斯先生。

Would you like a cup of tea or coffee?
您願意喝茶呢，還是喝杯咖啡？

Can I get you some coffee?
您要喝咖啡嗎？

Can I get you something to drink?
您要喝點什麼嗎？

Would you give me your business card [1]?
能給我一張名片嗎？

Please make yourself comfortable [2].
請不要拘束！

Phrase List

★**sit down**　坐下

Why don't you sit down for a while?

你怎麼不稍坐片刻？

★**something to drink**　可以喝的飲料

Would you like something to drink?

您要喝點什麼嗎？

★**make comfortable**　安逸自在

We tried to make our guests comfortable.

我們盡力讓我們的客人感到舒服自在。

Phrase List

Word Bank

1. **business card**　名片
2. **make yourself comfortable**　不要拘束

Word Bank

MP3 084

Lesson 4 引導訪客方位

Please come on in.
請進！

Just follow [1] me, please.
請跟我來。

你也可以這麼說：
◆This way, please.
請走這裡。

Mr. White's office is just through those doors.
懷特先生的辦公室穿過那些門就到了。

Please take the elevator [2] on your left to the seventh floor.
請搭您左手邊的電梯到七樓。

This is our conference room.
這是我們的會議室。

That is our Vice President's office.
那是我們副總裁的辦公室。

Phrase List

★**come on** 跟著來

You'd better go now, and I'll come on later.

你最好現在就去，我隨後就到。

★**follow sbdy.** 跟隨某人

David follows me to school.

大衛跟著我去上學。

★**on the+序號+floor** 在第…樓層

We live on the third floor.

我們住在三樓。

Phrase List

Word Bank

1. follow *v.* 跟隨

2. elevator *n.* 電梯

Word Bank

MP3 085

Lesson 5 說明主管的現況

Mr. Johnson is expecting[1] you.
強生先生正在等您來。

Mr. Johnson can see you now.
強生先生現在可以見您。

Mr. Johnson is in conference.
強生先生正在開會。

Mr. Johnson is in the middle of something[2].
強生先生正在忙。

Mr. Johnson cannot see you now.
強生先生現在無法見您。

I am sorry, but Mr. Johnson is not in now.
抱歉，但是強生先生現在不在。

Mr. Johnson will be here very soon.
強生先生很快就會來了。

Mr. Johnson will see you in a minute[3].
強生先生馬上就會來見你了。

Phrase List

★**expect sbdy.** 期盼某人

We'll expect you for dinner.

我們會等你吃晚餐。

★**in the middle of something** 忙碌於某事

I'm in the middle of something.

我現在正在忙。

★**in a minute** 馬上

I'll be back in a minute.

我馬上就回來。

Word Bank

1. **expect** *v.* 期待
2. **in the middle of something** 忙碌中
3. **in a minute** 馬上

MP3 086

Lesson 6

傳達轉告來訪

Let me call Mr. Johnson to come over.
我去叫強生先生過來。

I will call Mr. Johnson's office.
我會打電話到強生先生的辦公室。

I will tell Mr. Johnson you are here.
我會告訴強生先生您來了！

Let me see if Mr. Johnson is available.
我看看強生先生有沒有空。

Please wait for a moment. I will inform Mr. Johnson that you're here.
請等一下，我來通知強生先生你的來訪。

Mr. Smith, Mr. White is expecting you.
史密斯先生，懷特先生正在等您來！

I will inform Mr. Johnson right now.
我現在馬上通知強生先生。

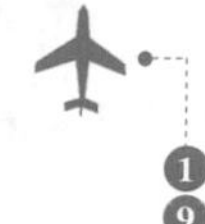

Phrase List

★**come over** 過來

Come over any time; I'm always in.

任何時間都可以過來，我總是在家的。

Why don't you come over with John?

你為什麼不和約翰一起來？

Phrase List

MP3 087

Lesson 7 問候客戶

How are you?

你好嗎？

Hi, John, what have you been doing?

嗨，約翰，最近都在忙些什麼？

你也可以這麼說：

◆How do you do?

你好嗎？

How's everything going?

一切都好嗎？

How have you been?

近來好嗎？

On behalf of [1] our company, I would like to welcome [2] all of our visitors.

我代表本公司歡迎各位來訪。

Phrase List

★**on behalf of** 代表…

I am calling on behalf of Mr. White.

謹此代表懷特先生。

Word Bank

1. on behalf of 代表

2. welcome v. 歡迎

MP3 088

Lesson 8
和訪客寒暄

How was your flight?
您一路上順利吧？

Have you recovered [1] from the journey [2]?
是否已從旅途的疲勞中回復過來？

How long do you intend [3] to stay in the USA?
您打算在美國停留多久？

What's the main [4] purpose [5] of your visit?
您來訪的主要目的是什麼？

What do you think of Taiwan?
您對台灣的印象如何？

I hope you had a good sleep last night.
希望您昨晚睡得好。

I have longed to meet you.
久仰大名。

Phrase List

★**think of** 想法

What do you think of this project?

對這個計畫你有什麼想法？

★**last night** 昨晚

I went to see a movie last night.

我昨天去看電影。

Phrase List

Word Bank

1. **recover** *v.* 復原
2. **journey** *n.* 旅行
3. **intend** **v.** 企圖
4. **main** **a.** 主要的
5. **purpose** **n.** 目的

Word Bank

MP3 089

Lesson 9 結束招待

Thank you for coming.
感謝來訪。

Have a nice day.
祝你有美好的一天。

Have a good night.
祝你晚上愉快。

Good night.
晚安！（道別用語）

Let's get together [1] again sometime.
有空再找個時間聚一聚。

Thank you for everything.
感謝您所做的一切。

Phrase List

★**have** 擁有

Have a good day.

祝你有美好的一天。

★**get together** 聚會

When can we get together?

我們什麼時候要聚會？

Phrase List

Word Bank

1. get together 聚會

Word Bank

MP3 090

Lesson 10

行程安排

Where do you want to visit[1] tomorrow morning?

明天上午您想要去哪裡參訪？

What is your opinion[2] about the schedule of the next six days?

接下來的六天行程您有何意見？

What do you say of 10 o'clock on the morning of the 22nd?

二十二日早上十點您看怎樣？

What do you think of this arrangement[3]?

這樣的安排您覺得怎樣？

What about the following[4] Wednesday? How is that?

接下的週三如何？您覺得呢？

Is there anything else you'd like to achieve[5] on this visit?

這次來訪你們還有其他事要處理嗎？

Can we make it on Wednesday next week?

我們可以安排在下週三嗎？

Phrase List

★**say** 說、假定

How do you say this in English?

這在英語中怎麼說？

Let's say you miss the plane, what do you plan to do?

假使你趕不上飛機，你準備怎麼辦？

Phrase List

Word Bank

1. **visit** *v.* 拜見、參觀
2. **opinion** *n.* 意見
3. **arrangement** *n.* 安排
4. **following** *a.* 接下來的
5. **achieve** *v.* 完成

Word Bank

MP3 091

Lesson 11

出席行程

I am not certain [1] if I will be free on that day.

我還不確定那一天是否有空。

I would love to meet you for lunch and talk things over.

我很樂意與你共進午餐並洽談業務。

Thank you for taking all the trouble to arrange the schedule for my visit.

感謝您費心安排我的來訪行程。

I'll be very happy to join you.

我很樂意參加。

We all will be most delighted [2] to go and meet him.

我們非常高興去拜見他。

Then I'll come for you at 2:00 this afternoon.

我會在下午兩點去接你。

We'll be waiting for you in the lobby[3] downstairs[4].

我們會在樓下的大廳等你。

Phrase List

★**talk over** 商議

We need to talk the project over.

我們需要討論這個企畫案。

★**wait for** 等待

I'll be waiting for you.

我會等你。

Phrase List

Word Bank

1. **certain** *a.* 無疑的
2. **delighted** *a.* 高興的
3. **lobby** *n.* 大廳
4. **downstairs** *adv.* 在樓下

Word Bank

Lesson 12

安排會議

Let's kick off[1] the meeting at 10 o'clock.
我們十點鐘召開會議。

I will arrange a staff[2] meeting.
我會安排一場員工會議。

Can we set[3] the date for the next meeting?
我們可以安排下一次會議的日期嗎？

So, the next meeting will be on next Monday.
所以下一次的會議會在下星期一。

I'll make a reservation and confirm the date by e-mail.
我會預約並用電子郵件確認日期。

We can hold the meeting[4] in Room 301.
我們會在 301 會議室召開會議。

We will fix a meeting[5] next week to discuss the project budget.
我們會在下週安排討論計畫預算會議。

When will you be available?

你什麼時候有空？

Phrase List

★**kick off** 開始

Let's kick off the discussion at three pm.

我們下午三點開始討論。

★**set the date** 安排日期

Let's set the date on the morning of the 22nd.

我們日期安排在二十二日早上。

★**hold the meeting** 召開會議

We decided to hold the meeting next week.

我們決定在下週召開會議。

Phrase List

Word Bank

1. **kick off** 開始
2. **staff** *n.* 員工
3. **set** *v.* 安排
4. **hold the meeting** 舉行會議
5. **fix a meeting** 舉行會議

Word Bank

MP3 093

Lesson 13

邀請客戶

Will you come along with me?
您願意和我一起來嗎？

Would you like to join us?
您要加入我們嗎？

Do you have any plans on Sunday night?
您週日晚上有任何計畫嗎？

Will you be free on this Friday?
您本週五是否有空？

Mr. Jones invites you to attend our annual party.
瓊斯先生邀請您出席我們的年度宴會。

Why don't you join us? Come on. That would be fun.
何不加入我們？來嘛！一定會很好玩。

Would you like to have dinner with us?
要不要和我們一起吃晚餐？

通常你會聽到對方這麼回答：

◆Yes, I would love to.

好啊！我很想去。

◆I would love to, but I have other plans.

我很想去，但是我有其他計畫了！

Phrase List

★**come along**　一起

Jason came along with us.

傑森和我們一起來的。

★**join sbdy.**　加入某人陣容

Come on, join us.

來嘛，加入我們吧！

Phrase List

MP3 094

Lesson 14

參觀公司

Let me show you our office.
我帶你們參觀我們辦公室。

Would you be interested in visiting BCQ Company?
您是否有興趣參觀BCQ公司？

Would you want to visit one or two of our factories?
您要不要參觀一兩家我們的工廠？

Is it possible for you to visit our factories if this won't cause you too much trouble?
如果不太麻煩的話，要不要參觀我們的工廠呢？

This is our sales marketing department.
這是我們的市場行銷部門。

That is Mr. White's office.
那是懷特先生的辦公室。

Down there is our conference room.
盡頭那是我們的會議室。

Our staff is working all around here.
我們的人員都在這裡工作。

Phrase List

★**show sbdy. sthg.** 展示某物給某人看

Let me show you this.
來看這個東西。

★**cause trouble** 製造麻煩

He caused so much trouble.
他製造了很多麻煩事。

MP3 095

Lesson 13

安排觀光行程

John will accompany you during your stay in Taiwan.

在您停留台灣期間，約翰將會和您同行。

I am in charge of taking you to the scenic spots [1].

我負責帶您到觀光景點參觀。

Any special places you want to go?

有沒有特別想去的地方？

Would you like to go sightseeing [2] tomorrow?

您明天想去觀光嗎？

Would you like to see temples?

您想看寺廟嗎？

Where would you like to visit?

您想去哪裡拜訪？

What scenic spots have you been to?

您去過哪些觀光景點？

How about going to Taipei 101?

去台北 101 大樓怎麼樣？

Phrase List

★**during**+名詞（時間、 行程）

在某段時間內

Call me sometime during the holidays.

假期時間有空的話打電話給我。

★**in charge of** 負責…

He's not allowed to be left alone in charge of this work.

他不准單獨留在此地負責這份工作。

Word Bank

1. scenic spot 觀光景點

2. go sightseeing 去觀光

MP3 096

Lesson 16

購買紀念商品

Do you want to buy some souvenirs for your family?

您要為家人買一些紀念品嗎？

What kind of souvenirs do you want to buy?

您想要買哪一類的紀念品？

There is a night market nearby[1].

附近有一個夜市。

It's just around the corner[2].

就在附近。

Would you like to go shopping[3]?

您要不要去購物？

There is a souvenir market about a ten-minute walk away.

只要十分鐘路程就有一個賣紀念品的市場。

I recommend[4] you to go to Shih-lin night market.

我建議您去士林夜市。

We are planning to go shopping tonight.
我們安排今晚去購物。

Phrase List

★around the corner 在附近

The hospital is around the corner.

醫院就在附近。

★go shopping 去購物

Let's go shopping tonight.

我們今天晚上去逛街購物。

★**about** 大約

It's about time to leave.

該離開了。

Word Bank

1. **nearby** *adv.* 附近
2. **around the corner** 在附近
3. **go shopping** 去購物
4. **recommend** *v.* 建議

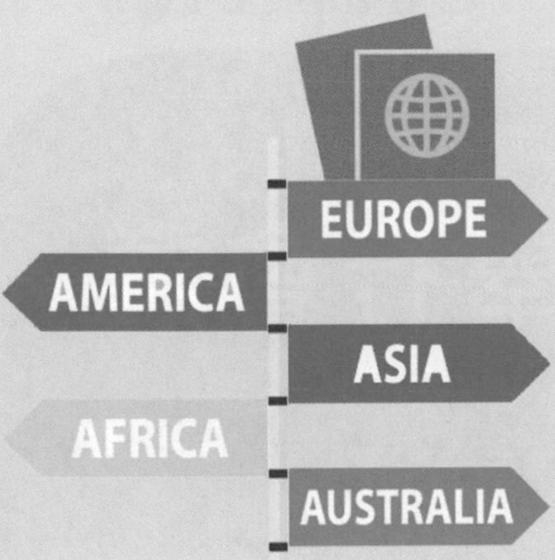
EUROPE
AMERICA
ASIA
AFRICA
AUSTRALIA

EUROPE
AMERICA
ASIA
AFRICA
AUSTRALIA

Chapter 9

舉行會議

097

Lesson 1

開場白

Good morning/afternoon, everyone.

大家早安/午安！

Welcome, everyone.

歡迎各位！

I am so glad to see everyone here on time.

很高興看見各位準時出席。

I'd like to thank David and Sophia for coming over from Taiwan.

感謝大衛和蘇菲亞遠從台灣而來。

Thank you all for attending.

謝謝你們參加（會議）

Unfortunately [1], Mr. Baker will not be with us today.

很遺憾貝克先生今天無法出席(會議)。

This is my first time to attend this conference [2].

這是我第一次參加這個會議。

Thank you for inviting us.

謝謝你們邀請我們。

Phrase List

★**someone's**+序號+**time**　某人的第幾次

Today is my first time to attend the party.

今天是我第一次參加宴會。

This is her second time to borrow "the Little Women."

這是她第二次借小婦人這本書。

Word Bank

1. unfortunately *adv.* 不幸地

2. attend this conference 參加會議

MP3 098

Lesson 2

宣佈會議開始

Let's begin, shall we?
(會議)開始，好嗎？

Let's begin.
(會議)開始了！

We'd better start.
我們最好開始（開會議）。

OK, let's get started.
好了，我們開始吧！

It's time to begin.
開始（討論）的時間到了。

你也可以這麼說：
◆It's about time to begin.
(會議的)時間到了。

Shall we begin?
開始好嗎？

Let's get down to business.

開始討論正事了。

If we are all here, let's start the meeting.

如果全都到齊，會議就開始。

Phrase List

★**Let's+**原形動詞　讓我們做某事

Let's kick off the meeting.

會議開始。

★**time to+**原形動詞　做某事的時間

It's time to finish your homework.

該是你寫完功課的時候了。

★**get down to**　開始認真對待…

He got down to his work after the holidays.

假期之後，他開始專心工作。

MP3 099

Lesson 3

責任分配

Who will keep the minutes?

誰要做會議記錄？

Susan has agreed to take the minutes [1].

蘇姍答應要做會議紀錄。

Debby, would you mind taking the minutes for the meeting?

黛比，妳介意做會議記錄嗎？

Maria, would you mind taking notes [2] today?

瑪麗亞，妳介意記錄今天的備忘錄嗎？

John has agreed to give us a report on this meeting.

約翰同意要給我們一份有關會議的報告。

David will lead point 1, Joy point 2, and Mr. White point 3.

大衛要主持第一點，喬伊第二點，懷特先生第三點。

The chairperson is ill, so I am speaking on behalf of him.

主席病了，因此我代表他發言。

Phrase List

★**keep the minutes** 會議記錄

I'll keep the minutes for you.

我會幫你做會議記錄。

★**agree to**+原形動詞 同意做某事

I agree to take the responsibility.

我答應要負責任。

Phrase List

Word Bank

1. **take the minutes** 擔任會議記錄
2. **note n.** 備忘錄

Word Bank

MP3 100

Lesson 4 議程安排

On the agenda, you'll see there are four items.
在議程上，你會看見有四個議題。

Our agenda has three items. They are...
我們的議程有三個議題，分別是…

First..., second..., finally....
第一個是…，第二個是…，最後一個是…

Do you all have a copy of the agenda?
你們都有一份今天的議程嗎？

Has everyone received a copy of the annual project?
每個人都有收到一份年度計畫嗎？

Let's preview the agenda.
我們先看一下議程。

I suggest we follow the agenda.
我建議我們依這個議程（討論）。

If you don't mind, I'd like to go in order today.
如果各位不介意，今天就照順序討論。

Let's skip item 1 and move on to item 2.
我們跳過議程一，直接進行議程二。

I suggest we take item 2 last.
我建議我們最後再討論議程二。

Phrase List

★**a copy of**+名詞　某物的副本

Send me a copy of your price list.
寄一份你們的報價單副本給我。

★**in order**　按順序

The cards are in order.
撲克牌有按照順序。

★**move on**　前進

Let's move on and get back to the material.
我們繼續回到材料的主題上。

MP3 101

Lesson 5

會議時間

There will be five minutes for each item.

每一個議題有五分鐘（時間）。

We'll have to keep each item to 15 minutes.

每個議題將進行十五分鐘。

Everybody has five minutes for each idea.

每一個人有五分鐘的時間說明每個點子。

The meeting will last one hour.

會議將進行一個小時。

I hope the meeting can be finished by 4 o'clock.

我希望會議可以在四點結束。

The meeting will finish at three o'clock.

會議將進行到三點。

The meeting should finish by lunch time.

會議應該在午餐前就結束。

The meeting should take about forty minutes.

會議將花大約四十分鐘。

Let's aim for a 3:00 finish.

讓我們預計在三點結束。

Phrase List

★**each**+名詞 每一個

Each boy gets a present.

每個男孩得到一份禮物。

★**last** 持續

How long will the meeting last?

會議要開多久?

Phrase List

MP3 102

Lesson 6

會議主題

Now we come to the question of the pricing policy.

現在我們進行有關價格策略的問題。

So, the first item on the agenda is our program.

所以啦，議程上的第一個議題是有關我們程式。

I'd suggest we start with the advertisement [1].

我建議我們從廣告開始。

We are here today to discuss how we can improve [2] the program.

我們今天在這裡要討論如何更新我們的程式。

I'd like to make sure that we come to an agreement [3] about the annual plan.

今天，我要確定我們已經針對年度計畫達成共識。

Our main aim today is to talk about the design[4] of the summer catalogue.

我們今天的主要目的是討論夏季型錄的設計。

The reason we are here today is to discuss our promotion plans.

我們今天在這裡的原因是要討論促銷計畫。

Phrase List

★**start with+**名詞　從某事物開始

Where to start with the advertisement?

要從廣告的哪裡開始？

★**come to an agreement**　達成共識

Did we come to an agreement?

我們有達成共識嗎？

Word Bank

1. advertisement *n.* 廣告

2. improve *v.* 改進

3. agreement *n.* 同意

4. design *n.* 設計

103

Lesson 7 議題討論

Shall we get down to business?
要不要就主題來討論？

Can you tell us how the sales project is progressing?
你可以告訴我們銷售計畫的進度如何嗎？

How is the CSR project coming along?
客戶服務計畫進行得如何？

First, let's go over[1] the report.
首先，我們先瀏覽一遍報告。

Here are the minutes from our last meeting.
這裡有一份我們上次的會議記錄。

First of all, we have to discuss the pricing policy[2].
首先，我們必須討論價格策略。

If there is nothing else we need to discuss, let's move on to today's agenda.
如果沒有其他需要討論的，就繼續今天的議程。

Phrase List

★**come along** 進展

How does the project come along?

計畫進展得如何了？

★**go over** 瀏覽

I've got to go over my textbooks.

我必須要先瀏覽一遍我的課本。

★**first of all** 最重要的事

First of all, I've got to finish it on time.

首先，我必須要準時完成。

Word Bank

1. go over 瀏覽

2. policy n. 策略

MP3 104

Lesson 8 討論新議題

The next item is...
下一個議題是…

The final item is...
最後一個議題是…

Let's begin with the first item.
我們先從第一個議題開始討論。

Let's begin with the design.
我們先從設計開始討論。

Is there any discussion on this?
這個還有要討論的嗎？

Let's move on to the next item.
我們進行下一個議題。

If nobody has anything else to add [1], let's move to the next.
如果沒有要發言，我們進行下一個。

We have discussed the design, and what is next?
我們討論過設計了，下一個（要討論）是什麼？

The next item on today's agenda is our services [2].

今天議程的下一個議題是有關我們的服務。

Word Bank

1. **add** **v.** 增加
2. **service** **n.** 服務

MP3 105

Lesson 9 腦力激盪

Don't hold back.

儘管說出來不要保留。

I have got an idea.

我有一個點子。

I have a few ideas I'd like to share with you.

我有一些點子，希望和各位分享。

I've called this meeting to brainstorm [1] ideas for effective promotion.

我召開這次會議，是希望為我們的促銷做一些腦力激盪。

All right, we have a lot of good ideas.

好了，我們有很多很好的點子。

We need some creative[2] ideas.

我們需要一些有創意的點子。

Here is my suggestion.

以下是我的建議。

Come on, guys, use your head[3].

拜託，各位，動動你們的腦袋。

Phrase List

★**hold back** 抑制

I am asking you to hold back your emotions.

我要求你壓抑你的情緒。

★**use someone's head** 要某人思考

Did you use your head?

你有動腦想一想嗎？

Word Bank

1. **brainstorm** *n.* 集思廣益
2. **creative** *a.* 創造性的
3. **use someone's head** 動動某人的腦袋

MP3 106

Lesson 10

鼓勵發言

Please go on.
請說下去。

Shall we start with Mr. Jones?
我們先從瓊斯先生開始好嗎？

Would you like to introduce [1] this item?
你要介紹這個議題嗎？

David, would you like to kick off?
大衛，可以從你開始嗎？

We can't all speak at once. One at a time.
我們無法人人都同時發言。一個一個來。

Would you like to open the discussion [2]?
你要先開始討論嗎？

What's on your mind [3]?
你的想法呢？

David, you've got to speak out.
大衛，你要說出實在的話啊！

Phrase List

★**go on** 繼續

If he goes on like this he'll lose his job.

如果他繼續這樣，是會丟掉工作的。

★**at once** 立刻

Do it at once!

馬上就做！

★**speak out** 仗義執言

Is there no one wants to speak out?

沒有人要仗義執言嗎？

Word Bank

1. **introduce** *v.* 介紹
2. **discussion** *n.* 討論
3. **on someone's mind** 某人的想法

MP3 107

Lesson 11

詢問意見

What do you suggest, Sophia?
蘇菲亞，妳的建議呢？

We need to go into this in more detail.
我們需要再仔細討論。

Could you elaborate [1] on your point?
你可以解釋一下你的重點嗎？

Any comments [2]?
有任何意見嗎？

I appreciate [3] your advice.
我很想聽聽您的意見。

It sounds good to me. What do you two think of it?
聽起來很不錯，你們兩位覺得怎樣？

Say something, gentlemen.
各位，說說話呀！

Good question.
好問題。

Phrase List

★**go into** 調查

I'll go into the matter.

我會調查這事的。

★**in detail** 細節地

I'll show you it in detail.

我會將細節展示給你看。

★**sound+**形容詞 某事物聽起來...

It sounds great. I'll try this one.

聽起來很棒。我要試這一個。

Word Bank

1. **elaborate** *v.* 詳盡闡述
2. **comment** *n.* 建議、意見
3. **appreciate** *v.* 感激

MP3 108

Lesson 12 發表個人言論

In my opinion, ...
依我的觀念，…

Personally, I think ...
依個人的觀念，我認為，…

I have a point to add[1].
我有一個重點要補充。

Could I comment[2] on that?
我能就這點發表言論嗎？

I'd like to show you my point.
我要說明一下我的論點。

But I have to explain[3].
但是我一定要解釋一下。

According to[4] our new research, ...
根據我們的最新研究，…

Actually, I have no idea about it.
其實我對這件事一點也不知道。

Phrase List

★**in someone's opinion** 某人的觀念

In my opinion, Taiwan is a beautiful place.

依我的觀念，台灣是一個漂亮的地方。

★**according to** 根據…

According to the newest studies, we have to place an order.

根據最新的研究，我們應該要下訂購單。

Word Bank

1. **add** *v.* 補充
2. **comment** *v.* 發表意見
3. **explain** *v.* 解釋
4. **according to** 根據

MP3 109

Lesson 13

會議上插話

May I have a word?
我能說話嗎？

Excuse me for interrupting [1].
抱歉，我要插話。

Excuse me, may I ask for clarification [2] on this?
抱歉，我能在這一點上做個說明嗎？

Sorry, but we'd like to hear some other views on this item.
抱歉，但是我們希望聽聽在這一點上的其他意見。

Just a moment. Can we come back to you later?
請稍等。我們能夠等一下再回到你的議題上嗎？

Sorry to interrupt, can we let Mark finish?
抱歉插話，我們可以讓馬克先說完嗎？

I have a question.
我有一個問題。

May I ask a question?

我能問一個問題嗎？

Phrase List

★**have a word**　簡短一句話

Let's have a word with her.

我們應該要和她說句話。

★**excuse me for**+動名詞　抱歉我做某事

Excuse me for changing my mind.

抱歉，我要改變想法。

★**just a moment**　稍等片刻

Just a moment. Let me take a look at it

請稍等一下。讓我看一下。

Word Bank

1. **interrupt** *v.* 打斷(講話或講話人)
2. **clarification** *n.* 澄清

Phrase List

Word Bank

MP3 110

Lesson 14
繼續會議

Shall we continue?
繼續（進行討論）好嗎？

Let's come back to this issue [1].
我們再回到這個議題上。

I think we've covered everything.
我認為我們已經涵蓋到每一件事了。

It looks as though we've covered the main items.
看來我們已經都討論過主要議題了。

Shall we leave that item?
這個議題要不要就到此結束？

Why don't we move on to the third item instead [2]?
我們為什麼不先改為進行第三個議題？

Is there any other business?
還有其他事嗎？

Is there anything else to discuss?
還有沒有任何要討論的？

Phrase List

★**shall**+主詞+原形動詞　是否可以…

Shall we come over?

我們可以過來嗎？

★**cover everything**　涵蓋每件事

Does it cover everything at all?

到底有沒有涵蓋到每一件事？

★**leave**　棄之不理

Shall we leave this point?

這個主題要不要就此結束？

Word Bank

1. **issue** *n.* 問題
2. **instead** *ad.* 作為替代

MP3 111

Lesson 15

結束議題

That's everything on the agenda.
這就是議程上所有的事了。

That's enough[1] for this item now.
這個議題討論到現在也夠了。

That's all for our summer promotion.
有關夏季促銷就這些囉！

I'll have to bring this point to a close[2].
這個議題就先結束囉！

I guess[3] nobody has anything else to say.
我猜沒有人有其他事要說吧！

We'll leave this point now and move on to the next item.
現在這一點就先這樣，我們先進行下一個議題。

That's enough for this item.
這個議題討論到此就夠了。

Phrase List

★**be enough for** 對...而言是足夠的

That's enough for me.

這個對我來說是足夠的。

★**anything+**形容詞　任何事...

Do you have anything else to tell me?

你有任何事要告訴我嗎？

Phrase List

Word Bank

1. enough *a.* 足夠的

2. close **n.** 結束

3. guess *v.* 猜測

Word Bank

MP3 112

Lesson 16

總結

Let me just summarize [1] my ideas.
讓我總結我的點子。

Before we close, I will summarize the main points.
在結束前，我來將要點做個總結。

Let me quickly summarize what we've done today.
讓我快速總結一下今天討論的！

Let me go over today's main points.
讓我很快地再確認今天的重點。

To sum up [2], send our clients the latest catalogue.
總而言之，要寄給我們的客戶最新的型錄。

To sum up, we'll offer this position to him.
總而言之，我們要提供這個職位給他。

In brief [3], we have to cut costs [4] by one third.
總而言之，我們必須要將成本削減三分之一。

We have made good progress [5] today.
我們今天很有進展。

We'll carry on our discussion tomorrow.
我們明天將繼續討論。

Phrase List

★**sum up** 總而言之

To sum up, I've got to arrive at five pm.

總而言之，我必須要在下午五點到達。

★**in brief** 簡而言之

In brief, you are my last chance.

簡而言之，你是我的最後機會。

★**make progress** 進步

You've made good progress since then.

從那時候至今，你進步很多。

Word Bank

1. **summarize** *v.* 總結
2. **sum up** 總而言之
3. **in brief** 總而言之
4. **cut cost** 縮減成本
5. **progress** *n.* 進步

MP3 113

Lesson 17 詢問對會議的瞭解

Do you understand everything?
你們都明白嗎？

Is everything clear [1]?
每個人都清楚嗎？

Does anyone have any questions?
還有人有任何問題嗎？

Does everyone agree with [2] this?
每一個人都同意這一點嗎？

Is there anything I can clarify [3]?
還有其他我可以澄清的嗎？

Shall I go over the main points?
我可以再確認一次重點嗎？

Any final questions?
還有任何最後的問題嗎？

Are we agreed [4]?
大家同意嗎？

Phrase List

★**agree** 同意

Do you agree?

你同意嗎？

★**agree with**和...意見一致

I agree with Tom's statement.

我同意湯姆的說明。

Word Bank

1. **clear** *a.* 清楚的
2. **agree with...** 同意…
3. **clarify** *v.* 澄清
4. **agreed** *a.* 意見一致的

MP3 114

Lesson 18

宣佈散會

We'll stop [1] here for today.
今天就到這裡結束。

Let's finish here.
今天就到這裡結束。

Let's call it a day [2].
今天就到這裡結束。

Let's bring this to a close for today.
今天的會議就到此結束。

If there are no other comments, the meeting is finished.
假如沒有其他意見，會議結束了。

Good, if there are no further points, we can finish here.
很好，如果沒有進一步的重點，我們今天就到這裡結束。

I declare the meeting adjourned [3].
我宣布散會。

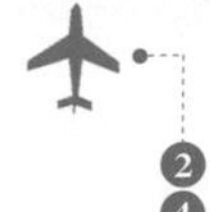

Phrase List

★call it a day （今天）到此結束

Let's call it a day. See you tomorrow.

今天就到這裡結束。明天見囉！

Word Bank

1. **stop** *v.* 結束
2. **call it a day** 今天到此結束
3. **adjourn** *v.* 休會

EUROPE
AMERICA
ASIA
AFRICA
AUSTRALIA

Chapter 10

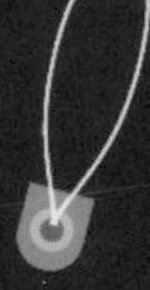

作簡報

MP3 115

Lesson 1 歡迎詞

Welcome, ladies and gentlemen.
各位先生、女士，歡迎。

Good morning, gentlemen.
各位先生，早安。

Good afternoon, everyone.
各位，午安。

Thank you for coming.
謝謝各位出席。

Are you ready?
大家準備好了嗎？

Is everyone here?
大家都到齊了嗎？

Please have a seat [1], ladies.
各位女士，請坐。

I am glad to see everyone is here.
很高興在此看到各位。

Phrase List

★**be ready** 準備好

I am ready.

我準備好了。

★**be here** 出席

Is Mr. Martin here?

馬汀先生到了嗎？

★**have a seat** 坐下

Please have a seat, ladies and gentlemen.

各位先生、女士，請坐。

Phrase List

Word Bank

1. have a seat 請坐

Word Bank

MP3 116

Lesson 2

開場白

I am going to talk about our CSR projects.
我是要來談論有關我們的客服計畫。

The purpose of my presentation [1] is to introduce annual projects.
我今天簡報的目的是要介紹年度計畫。

Does everyone have a copy of the sales report?
每個人都有一份銷售報告嗎？

I am eager to show you my ideas.
我迫不亟待要給各位看我的想法。

Today is a good opportunity [2] to accomplish [3] my purpose.
今天是一個完成我的目的的好機會。

I would like you to see what we have worked on for the last three months.
我要各位瞧瞧我們過去三個月努力的結果。

I am here to represent [4] our annual plans.
我今天要報告的是我們的年度計畫。

Phrase List

★**be eager to**+原形動詞　迫不亟待做某事

He's eager to meet his son.

他迫不亟待要和他的兒子見面。

★**work on**　致力於某事

I've worked on the project for 4 months.

我已經致力於這個企畫案四個月了。

Word Bank

1. **presentation** *n.* 簡報
2. **opportunity** *n.* 機會
3. **accomplish** *v.* 完成
4. **represent** *v.* 做告報

MP3 117

Lesson 3

簡報架構

I will begin by the latest[1] sales report.

我將用最新的銷售報告開始。

I'll start by describing the current[2] position in Europe.

我將從說明目前的在歐洲的定位開始。

Then I'll mention[3] some of the problems we've encountered[4].

然後我會提及一些我們面臨的問題。

After that I'll consider the possibilities for further growth[5] next year.

之後我會考慮明年成長的可能性。

Finally, I'll summarize my presentation.

最後我會總結我的簡報。

Before concluding with some recommendations, I need to know your ideas.

總結一些建議之前，我需要知道你們的想法。

Phrase List

★**Finally,** 最後

Finally, you'll be sorry.

最後你將會後悔。

★**before+**動名詞 在做某事之前

Before finding the truth, I've got to call her.

在找出事實之前，我必須要打電話給她。

Phrase List

Word Bank

1. **latest** *a.* 最新的
2. **current** *a.* 目前的
3. **mention** *v.* 提及
4. **encounter** *v.* 遭遇
5. **growth** *n.* 成長

Word Bank

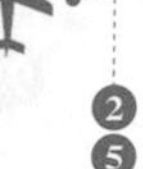

MP3 118

Lesson 4

簡報主題

The whole point of my representation is about profit.

我的簡報的宗旨就是有關利潤。

The goal for this presentation is to ensure you a good environment[1].

這次簡報的宗旨是要確保你們一個好的環境。

Then I'll move on to some of the achievements[2] we've made in Asia.

然後我會進行到我們在亞洲的一些成就。

After that I'll show you our opportunities in Africa.

之後，我會給各位看我們在非洲的機會。

Lastly, I'll quickly recap[3] before concluding with some recommendations[4].

最後，下結論之前，我會快速地總結之前的簡報。

That's all I have to say about Europe.
那是所有我要簡報有關歐洲的事。

Let's turn now to Asia.
現在我們開始進行亞洲的報告。

I will show you how we overcame[5] them.
我要向各位展示我們如何克服他們。

Phrase List

★that's all 全部

That's all you need to know about the price.
那是所有你需要知道關於價格的事。

★turn to （注意力）轉移至...

Please turn your attention to the plans
請把你的注意力放到計畫上。

Phrase List

Word Bank

1. **environment** *n.* 環境
2. **achievement** *n.* 成就
3. **recap** *v.* 重述要點
4. **recommendation** *n.* 建議
5. **overcome** *v.* 克服

Word Bank

MP3 119

Lesson 5

條列式說明

There are four points.

有四個重點。

I will show you one by one [1].

我會一個一個展示給各位看。

Firstly...secondly...thirdly...lastly...

首先…再來是…第三…最後…

First of all, I'll show you our proposal.

首先，我會展示給各位我們的計畫。

Then you will see lots of layouts [2].

然後你們會看見很多的版面。

After that, we supply [3] you with books and magazines

在這個之後，我們會提供給各位書籍和雜誌。

Finally, we need to make sure [4] which is much better.

最後，我們需要確定哪一個比較好。

Phrase List

★**one by one** 一個接著一個

One by one everyone has gone.

每個人一個個地不見了。

★**first of all** 首先、最重要

First of all, I'd like to thank you for your attention.

首先，我要感謝各位的注意。

★**supply sbdy. with sthg.** 提供某人某物

I'll supply you with my service.

我會提供給各位我的服務。

Phrase List

Word Bank

1. **one by one** 一個接著一個
2. **layout n.** 版面設計
3. **supply v.** 提供
4. **make sure** 確定

Word Bank

MP3 120

Lesson 6

提供發問

Do feel free to interrupt me if you have any questions.

如果有任何問題，請盡量發問。

I'll try to answer all of your questions after the presentation.

在簡報之後，我會試著回答你們的所有問題。

I plan to keep some time for questions after the presentation.

我打算在簡報之後留一些時間給各位發問。

Now I'll try to answer any questions you may have.

現在我會試著回答任何你們提出的問題。

Are there any questions?

還有任何問題嗎？

Do you have any questions?
你們還有任何問題嗎？

Are there any final questions?
最後還有問題嗎？

Phrase List

★feel free to+原形動詞 不要客氣去做某事

Please feel free to ask me any questions.

如果有任何問題，請盡量提出來問我。

★**try to**+原形動詞 試著去做某事

He tried to find out the answer to your questions.

他試著找出你的問題的答案。

121

Lesson 7

提供資料

Please turn to page 11.
請翻到第十一頁。

I want you to see the data [1] we have.
我要各位看看我們有的數據。

The forecasts [2] show that we would lose our orders.
預測顯示出我們將會失去訂單。

Each number on the chart [3] represents a result.
曲線圖上的每一個數字代表一個結果。

As you can see, here is our solution [4].
就各位所看到的，這是我們的解決方法。

Most of our clients don't like our products.
大部分我們的客戶不喜歡我們的產品。

BCQ Company sold two million cars last year.
BCQ公司去年已經賣出兩百萬輛車。

According to this report, we have to apologize to her.

根據這份報告，我們必須向她道歉。

Phrase List

★**turn to** 翻閱至、轉向

Everyone turn to page 11.

大家翻至第十一頁。

Word Bank

1. **data** *n.* 數據
2. **forecast** *n.* 預測
3. **chart** *n.* 圖表
4. **solution** *n.* 解決的方法

MP3 122

Lesson 8

說明研究報告

I've told you about the spring sales plans.
我已經告訴您有關春季銷售計畫了。

That's all I will say about the spring sales plans.
這就是我要談論的春季銷售計畫。

We've looked at his studies.
我們已經看過他的研究了。

Now we'll move on to No. 3.
現在我們進行到第三點。

Next is about the CSR system.
下一項是有關客服系統。

I'd like to discuss the new design.
我想要來討論新的設計。

Let's look at the whiteboard.
我們來看看白板。

What does this mean for SOP?
SOP是什麼意思？

Phrase List

Phrase List

★**look at sthg.** 端詳某物

Please look at the report.

請看報告。

★**mean for** 代表...意思

What does it mean for me?

這對我有什麼意思？

MP3 123

Lesson 9 細節説明

I will show you all the details.
我會展示給各位看所有的細節。

I'd likc to deal with this question later.
我想要稍後再討論這個問題。

I'll come back to this question later in my talk on annual sales plans.
等我論及年度銷售計畫時，再回到這個問題上。

I won't comment on this now.
我現在不想發表評論。

How do we make BCQ Company place an order[1] soon?
我們如何讓BCQ公司儘速下訂單？

We will solve every problem we encounter, right?
我們會解決每一個我們所遭遇的問題，對吧？

I will explain how the machine operates[2].
我會解釋這部機器如何運作。

Phrase List

★**place an order** 下訂單

We asked them to place an order.

我們要求他們下訂單。

★**solve problem** 解決問題

I'll solve all problems anyway.

不管如何，我會解決所有的問題。

Word Bank

1. **place an order** 下訂單
2. **operate v.** 運轉

MP3 124

Lesson 10

提出建議

Here is my advice.
以下是我的建議。

My recommendations are in two parts.
我的建議有兩大部分。

Therefore, I propose[1] the following strategy[2].
因此，我提出以下的策略。

I suggest we visit Taipei next week.
我建議我們下星期去參觀台北。

We offered him the computer for US$100.
這電腦我們向他開價一百美元。

My solution to this problem is a refund[3].
我對這個問題的建議是退費。

I give you some useful hints[4] on how to deal with[5] the matter.
我會就如何處理這件事給各位一些有益的指點。

I'll remind you of the main points we've considered.

我會提醒您我們已經考慮過的重點。

Phrase List

★**therefore** 因此

He was down with the flu, and therefore couldn't come to the party.

他患了流行性感冒，因此未能前來參加宴會。

★**solution to** 某事物的解決方式

The solution to your problem is making a decision.

對你的問題的解決方法是做出決定。

Word Bank

1. **propose** *v.* 提議
2. **strategy** *n.* 策略
3. **refund** *n.* 退費
4. **hint** *n.* 暗示
5. **deal with** 處理

MP3 125

Lesson 11

總結

I'd like to sum up now.
現在我要總結。

Let's sum up now, shall we?
讓我們來下結論好嗎？

Let's summarize briefly [1] what we've looked at.
我們簡短地總結一下我們看過的事項。

I would like to conclude with a picture.
我要用一張圖片作結論。

To conclude, BCQ Company will promise [2] to sell two million cars.
總結是，BCQ公司將會答應賣出兩百萬輛車。

Now to sum up how to improve our system.
要總結的是，如何加強我們的系統。

To summarize my points, you are the decision maker [3].
總結我的論點，你是做決定者。

In conclusion, I will do everything to satisfy[4] our customers.
結論是，我們將盡一切努力令我們的顧客滿意。

Phrase List

★**conclude with** 以...做出結論

I'd like to conclude with his statement.

我要用他的聲明做結論。

★**in conclusion** 結論是...

In conclusion, we'll do our best to finish it.

結論是，我們將盡力完成這件事。

Word Bank

1. **briefly** *adv.* 簡短地
2. **promise** *v.* 答應
3. **decision maker** 做決定者
4. **satisfy** *v.* 滿足

MP3 126

Lesson 12

結束簡報

Thank you, gentlemen.
感謝各位。

Thank you for being here today.
感謝各位今天的出席。

Thank you for your time.
感謝各位出席。

Thank you for your patience[1].
感謝各位的耐心（聽完簡報）。

Thank you very much for your attention[2].
感謝各位的專心（聽完簡報）。

Finally, let me remind you of some of the issues.
最後，我提醒你們一些事項。

If anyone still has questions, please let me know.
如果任何人還有問題，請讓我知道。

Phrase List

★**finally** 最後

Finally, he went home on May second.

最後，他在五月二日回家了。

★**remind sbdy. of sthg.** 提醒某人某事

I'll remind him of the shortage.

我會提醒他有關短缺的事。

Word Bank

1. **patience** *n.* 耐心
2. **attention** *n.* 注意力

Chapter 11

參加商展

MP3 127

Lesson 1

自我介紹

Hi, I am David Jones.
嗨，我是大衛・瓊斯。

My name is David. How can I help you?
我是大衛・瓊斯。需要我協助嗎？

This is my business card.
這是我的名片。

Let me introduce myself.
讓我自我介紹。

David Jones. Nice to meet you.
（我是）大衛・瓊斯。很高興認識你。

I am David Jones of BCQ Company.
我是BCQ公司的大衛・瓊斯。

I am the salesman of BCQ Company.
我是BCQ公司的業務。

I am general manager of BCQ Company.
我是BCQ公司的總經理。

Phrase List

★**introduce one's self** 某人介紹自己

Why don't you introduce yourself?

你怎麼不自我介紹一下？

Please introduce yourself to us.

請你向我們作自我介紹。

Let me introduce my co-worker to you.

讓我向你介紹一下我同事。

Lesson 2 介紹公司

We sell keyboards.

我們賣鍵盤。

We are a sports equipment[1] company.

我們是一家運動器材公司。

My company is doing business[2] with China.

我們公司跟中國做生意。

We often have business with Japanese.

我們常跟日本人做生意。

My company is an Internet company based in Taiwan.
我的公司是一家在台灣的網路公司。

Have you ever heard of BCQ?
您聽過BCQ嗎？

BCQ is a subsidiary company[3] of Intel.
BCQ是英特爾公司的子公司。

We are one of the subsidiary companies of IBM.
我們是IBM公司的其中一家子公司。

Phrase List

★**do business** 有生意往來

Do you do business with the USA?
你們和美國有生意上的往來嗎？

Word Bank

1. **equipment** *n.* 設備
2. **do business** 從事生意
3. **subsidiary company** 子公司

MP3 128

Lesson 3

參展術語

Let me show[1] you.
我展示給您看。

Let me show you something special.
我展示給您看一些特別的東西。

Would you like to take a look[2]?
您要看一看嗎？

Take a look at this.
看一下吧！

Are you interested in our products?
你對我們的產品感興趣嗎？

Do you want to try it?
您要試一試嗎？

What are you interested in?
你對什麼（產品）感興趣？

Let me explain this to you.
我來解釋給您聽。

Phrase List

★**show sbdy.** 向某人展示

Would you want me to show you?

需要我展示給您看嗎？

Would you show me your products?

可以請你展示你們的商品給我看嗎？

Let me show you this program.

讓我向你展示這個計畫。

Word Bank

1. **show** *v.* 展示
2. **take a look** 看一眼

MP3 129

Lesson 4

會場介紹商品

Do you want to know about our products?
您想了解一下我們的產品嗎？

We have several [1] kinds of keyboards.
我們有許多種鍵盤。

This item is popular [2].
這個商品很熱賣。

This set [3] includes a table and four chairs.
這一整組包括一張桌子和四張椅子。

This chair is made of wood.
這張椅子是木頭製的。

It is two feet high [4].
它有兩呎高。

It is one kilogram in weight [5].
它有一公斤重。

Phrase List

★**know about** 瞭解關於…

I'd like to know about your plans.

我想要瞭解你們的計畫。

★**be made of** 由…材質製成（成分不變）

The table is made of wood.

椅子是木頭製的。

★**be made from** 由…材質製成（成分改變）

The wine is made from grapes.

紅酒是由葡萄製成的。

Word Bank

1. **several** *a.* 幾個的
2. **popular** *a.* 受歡迎的
3. **set** *n.* 組
4. **high** *n.* 高度
5. **weight** *n.* 重量

MP3 130

Lesson 5 商品的優勢

You'll find our prices very favorable[1].
你會發現我們的價格非常優惠。

You'll find our prices most favorable.
你會發現我們的價格是最優惠。

I'm sure you'll find our price worth[2] accepting[3].
我相信你會發現我方的價格值得接受。

I will try my best to meet your requirements.
我會盡量滿足你們的需求。

You'll see that our prices are most attractive[4].
你會發現我方的價格極有競爭力。

Our product is lower priced than the competition[5].
我們產品價格低廉，具有競爭力。

Our product is competitive on the international market.

我們的產品在國際市場上具有競爭力。

Phrase List

★**find sthg.**+形容詞　發現某事物...

You'll find it convenient to work here.

你會發現在這裡工作很方便。

★**try someone's best**　盡某人的力量

I'll try my best to answer your questions.

我會盡量回答你的問題。

Phrase List

Word Bank

1. **favorable** *a.* 適合的
2. **worth** *a.* 有價值
3. **accept** *v.* 接受
4. **attractive** *a.* 具吸引力的
5. **competition** *n.* 競爭

Word Bank

MP3 131

Lesson 6

樣品

It's free.
免費的。

Help yourself.
請自取。

Free gift.
免費贈品。

We have some samples [1] in our showroom [2].
我們在展示間有一些樣本。

Could you provide [3] some samples free of charge?
能否免費提供一些樣品？

We can make a discount [4] on the samples.
我們有樣品可以打個折扣。

We can offer you free samples.
我們可以提供免費樣品給你。

They are not for sale.
它們是非賣品。

Phrase List

★**make a discount** 打折扣

Can you make a discount for me?

可以打個折扣給我嗎？

★**offer sbdy. sthg.** 提供某物給某人

I'll offer you a good chance.

我會提供一個好機會給你。

★**for sale** 販售

It's for sale.

這是要銷售的。

Word Bank

1. **sample** *n.* 樣品
2. **showroom** *n.* 展示房間
3. **provide** *v.* 提供
4. **discount** *n.* 折扣

MP3 132

Lesson 7

型錄

Free catalogue.
免費型錄。

I've brought a series of catalogues on our samples with me.
我帶來了一系列我們的樣本型錄。

Here are our price lists.
這是我們的價目單。

Here is our new catalogue.
這裡有我們新的型錄。

You'll find the required items, specifications [1] and quantities [2] all there.
你可以在上面知道所需的品項、規格和數量。

May I have a catalogue covering [3] your products?
能否給我一份你們商品的型錄？

May I have a copy of your catalogue?
可以給我一份你們的型錄嗎？

Do you have a catalogue of that item?
有那個品項的型錄嗎？

Phrase List

★**a series of** 一系列

They asked a series of questions.
他們問了我一系列的問題。

Word Bank

1. **specification** *n.* 詳述
2. **quantity** *n.* 數量
3. **cover** **v.** 包含

Lesson 8

詢價

Here's our inquiry [1] list.
這是我們的詢價單。

Could you give us some idea about your price?
你能介紹一下你們的價格嗎？

I'd like to have your lowest quotations [2], CIF Taipei.
我想請你們報到台北的最低價。

Would you please make your prices CIF including five percent [3]?
能請你報包括百分之五傭金在內的到岸價嗎？

Would you give me an offer for Item No.15?
你能給我第十五號商品的報價嗎？

May I have your offer of Model 612?
可以給我612型號商品的報價嗎？

Are all your quotations CIF?

你們所有的報盤都是到岸價嗎？

We can make them FOB if you like.

如果你要離岸價的話，我們可以報。

Phrase List

★**give sbdy. an idea**　讓某人瞭解

Please give me an idea what I shall do?

請讓我瞭解一下我該怎麼做。

★**give sbdy. an offer**　提供報價給某人

Would you give me an offer?

您能給我報價嗎？

Word Bank

1. **inquiry** *n.* 要求
2. **quotation** *n.* 報價
3. **percent** *n.* 百分比

MP3 134

Lesson 9

報價

Here is our latest price sheet.
這是我們最新的報價單。

Here is a detailed list of our offer.
這是我們的一份報價清單。

All the prices in the lists are subject to [1] our confirmation [2].
表上的價格以我方最後確認為準。

Our prices are on a CIF basis.
我們的報價都是成本加運費保險的到岸價格。

Do you quote [3] FOB or CIF?
你們是報離岸價還是到岸價？

But the offer is subject to immediate [4] acceptance [5].
但這個價格要立即接受才有效。

How long will you keep your offer valid [6]?
報價的有效期多長？

It will remain firm till Friday.

有效期到星期五為止。

Phrase List

★**be subject to** 以...為條件的

Our prices are subject to the plans.

我們的價格取決於計畫。

It is subject to the laws.

這是以法律為條件。

Phrase List

Word Bank

1. **be subject to** 以…為條件的
2. **confirmation** *n.* 確認
3. **quote** *v.* 報價
4. **immediate** *a.* 立即的
5. **acceptance** *n.* 接受
6. **valid** *a.* 有效的、合法的

Word Bank

MP3 135

Lesson 10

議價

It's too expensive[1].

太貴了！

No discount?

沒有折扣？

Could you give us some discount?

你能給我們一些折扣嗎？

What if my quantity is large?

如果我訂購的數量相當大呢？

How about a ten percent discount?

你覺得百分之十的折扣呢？

Could you givc us somc discount if my quantity is large?

如果我訂購的數量相當大，你能給我們一些折扣嗎？

I hope you'll quote us on your best terms.

希望按最優惠條件報價。

Phrase List

★**too+**形容詞　太...

Is it too late to call you now?

現在打電話給你會太晚嗎？

★**give a discount**　提供折扣

We'll give a special discount of 10 percent.

我們會給予九折的優待。

★**quote sbdy.**　提供報價給某人

I'll quote you again.

我會再給你報價。

Phrase List

Word Bank

1. expensive　*a.*　昂貴的

Word Bank

Lesson 11

交貨

How long does it usually take you to make delivery [1]?
你們通常多長時間交貨？

You have to deliver all goods by September 3.
你們必須在九月三日前交貨。

How do you deliver our products?
你們如何運送我們的商品？

We deliver all our orders within 2 months.
在二個月內我們就會全部交貨。

We guarantee [2] prompt [3] delivery of goods.
我們保證立即交貨。

We will make delivery on time.
我們會準時交貨。

The goods will be transported [4] to Taipei by air.
貨物將用空運送到台北。

I will send your goods by sea.
我會用海運運送你的商品。

Phrase List

★**within+數字+時間**　在某段時間內

I'll be home within 3 weeks.

我會在三個星期內回到家。

★**by air/sea**　海運/空運

Our products will be transported by air.

我們的商品將用空運運送。

Word Bank

1. **delivery** *v.* 運送
2. **guarantee** *v.* 保證
3. **prompt** *a.* 迅速的
4. **transport** **v.** 運輸

MP3 137

Lesson 12 庫存量

What about the supply[1] position[2]?
供應情況怎樣？

Do you think you will get any more in in a short time?
你們最近還會進貨嗎？

We want to find out if you can supply computers.
我們想知道你們能否供應電腦。

When will you get ready for the new supply?
什麼時候你們會有新貨供應？

For most of the articles[3] in the catalogue, we have good supply.
目錄中大部分的貨源都很充足。

Our old stock[4] has been entirely cleared out[5].
我們舊的存貨已全部出清。

We're sorry nothing is available at the moment.
很遺憾，目前無貨可供。

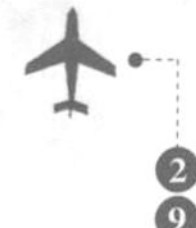

Phrase List

★**in a short time** 短時間內

You've made a lot of progress in a short time.

你短時間內進步神速。

★**clear out** 出清

We cleared out all our keyboards.

我們把所有的鍵盤出清。

Phrase List

Word Bank

1. **supply** n. 供應
2. **position** *n.* 現況
3. **article** *n.* 商品
4. **stock** *n.* 庫存
5. **clear out** 出空、出清

Word Bank

MP3 138

Lesson 13

對商品的評價

Pretty attractive [1] to us.
對我們很有吸引力。

It sounds good.
聽起來不錯。

They look very good.
看起來不錯！

I'm interested in No. 3 and No. 4.
我對三號和四號感興趣。

I'm interested in your hardware [2].
我對你們的硬體感興趣。

This is the one we're interested in.
我們對這一種比較感興趣。

If your prices are good, I can place an order right now.
如果你方價格合理，我可以馬上訂貨。

What's the size [3] of this product?
這個產品的尺寸是多少？

Phrase List

★**pretty+形容詞** 非常...

It's pretty easy to clear it up.

要清理是很簡單的。

★**look+形容詞** 看起來...

It looks perfect to me.

對我來說太完美了。

★**size of sthg.** 某物品的尺寸

What's the size of this shirt?

這件襯衫的尺寸是多少？

Word Bank

1. **attractive a.** 有吸引力的
2. **hardware n.** 硬體
3. **size n.** 尺寸

MP3 139

Lesson 14

商品的需求

What's your specifications [1]?

你們的規格是什麼？

We also need a lot of keyboards.

我們也需要很多量的鍵盤。

I'm thinking about buying some keyboards.

我想訂購一些鍵盤。

Would you accept orders according to our patterns [2]?

能否接受根據我們的樣式的訂貨？

All of our products meet your requirements.

所有我們的商品都符合你們的需要。

We are thinking of placing an order.

我們正在考慮訂貨。

I would like to get some idea of your shoes.

我想瞭解一下有關你們鞋子的情況。

What kind of literature[3] exactly? Leaflets or booklets?

你要什麼樣的確實資料？說明書還是小冊子？

Phrase List

★**think about**+動名詞　思考要做某事

I'm thinking about changing my thoughts.

我正想要改變我的想法。

★**think of**+動名詞　考慮要做某事

I'm thinking of joining a club.

我正考慮要參加俱樂部。

Word Bank

1. **specification** *n.* 規格
2. **pattern** *n.* 樣本
3. **literature** **n.** 印刷物

MP3 140

Lesson 15

數量的需求

How many pieces do you want?
你要多少數量？

It's an attractive quantity[1], isn't it?
數量很吸引人，不是嗎？

Running shoes are in high demand[2] these days.
最近運動鞋的需求量很大。

I will order 8000 pieces.
我會訂八千件。

Can I have your specific[3] inquiry?
可否告知您的詳細需求？

Would you tell us what quantity you have?
能否請你告知我方你的需求數量？

We need 100 sets of that model.
那一款我們需要一百套。

Phrase List

★**in high demand** 需求量很大

It is in high demand during this year.

今年的需求量很大。

★**these days** 近日

How are you these days?

您近來如何？

Word Bank

1. **quantity n.** 數量
2. **demand n.** 需求
3. **specific a.** 詳細的

MP3 141

Lesson 16 對市場的評價

How is the fur market?
皮貨市場如何？

Well, it's not very brisk [1].
並不太景氣。

But the selling season [2] is getting near.
不過銷售旺季就要到了。

You know the market has become very competitive [3].
你知道的，市場的競爭變得很激烈。

I think some of the items will find a ready market in Canada.
我覺得有些商品在加拿大會有銷路。

When the next supply comes in, we'll let you know.
等下一批貨到貨時，我們就會讓你知道。

Phrase List

★**a brisk sale** 暢銷

Our products are in a brisk sale all over the world.

我們的產品在全球是暢銷的。

★**selling season** 銷售旺季

So expanding the selling season is reasonable.

所以期待銷售旺季是合理的。

★**a ready market** 暢銷

Your hats can find a ready market in the USA.

你的帽子在美國會暢銷。

Word Bank

1. **brisk** *a.* 興旺的
2. **selling season** *n.* 銷售季節
3. **competitive** *a.* 具競爭性的

MP3 142

Lesson 17

客套用語

What can I do for you?
有什麼我幫得上忙嗎？

你也可以這麼說：
◆May I help you?
需要我協助嗎？

Just let me know if you need help.
如果需要我的協助，請告訴我。

If possible, I will place some orders.
如果可能的話，我會順便訂購一些貨。

This way, please.
請到這裏來。

Where is your office?
你們的辦公室在哪？

How late are you open?
你們營業到幾點？

All these items have been checked up.
所有項目都已核對過了。

Phrase List

★**if possible** 如果可能

Can you write down this, if possible?
如果可能的話，你可以寫下來嗎？

★**check up** 核對

Please check up the data.
請核對一下數據。

Phrase List

MP3 143

Lesson 18

套交情用語

Would you care to sit down for a while [1]?
您要不要坐一會呢？

Would you like to see it?
您要不要看？

Would you care for a drink?
您要不要來點兒喝的？

You should take advantage [2] of it.
您應該好好利用這個優勢。

You should give it a try [3].
您應該試一試。

Would you tell me your phone number?
您能告訴我您的電話號碼嗎？

I'll call you for another talk.
我會打電話給您再談。

You'll be hearing from us!
我們會很快給你們答覆的。

Please call again any time you like.
請隨時再打電話給我。

Phrase List

★**care to**+原形動詞　想要做某事

Would you care to have a look?

您要不要看一眼呢？

★**care for**+名詞 想要某物

Would you care for a cup of tea?

您要不要喝杯茶呢？

Word Bank

1. **for a while** 一陣子
2. **advantage** *n.* 優勢
3. **give it a try** 嘗試

MP3 144

Lesson 19 推託用語

Let me figure it out [1].
讓我算一下。

Let me put it this way.
讓我這麼說吧。

I'll have to ask my boss first.
我必須先問一下我的老闆。

There would be no problem, I suppose [2].
我想這毫無問題。

I don't catch your question [3].
我沒聽清楚你的問題。

Could you speak slower?
你能說得慢一點嗎？

Can you give me some feedback[4]?

你能給我一些建議嗎？

I'll remember that.

我會記住。

Phrase List

★**figure out** 理解、算出

I can't figure it out.

我算不出來。

★**put it this way** 如此解釋

We may put it this way.

我們可以這麼說。

★**catch+W**子句 理解…

I didn't catch what you said.

我沒有聽清楚你說的話。

Phrase List

Word Bank

1. figure it out 理解

2. suppose *v.* 推測

3. catch your question 理解你的問題

4. feedback *n.* 回應

Word Bank

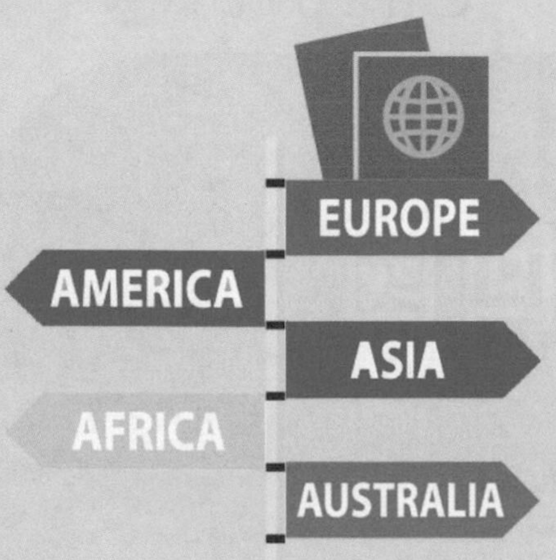
EUROPE
AMERICA
ASIA
AFRICA
AUSTRALIA

EUROPE
AMERICA
ASIA
AFRICA
AUSTRALIA

Chapter 12

MP3 145

Lesson 1

道別

Goodbye.

再見！

See you later.

待會見。

你也可以這麼說：

◆See you around.

待會見。

See you at 10 o'clock.

十點鐘碰面。

See you in the lounge.

大廳裡碰面。

See you Sunday.

星期日見。

你也可以這麼說：

◆See you tomorrow.

明天見。

See you again next week.

下星期再見。

I think I should be going.

我想我要走了。

I hate to say goodbye.

我討厭說再見。

It was really fun hanging out with you.

跟你相處真是有意思。

Phrase List

★**see you**　再見

See you soon.

再見。

★**at+**點鐘　在...點鐘

I'll be home at ten.

我十點鐘會在家。

★**hang out**　打發時間

Do you usually hang out with Americans?

你有經常和美國人在一起嗎？

Phrase List

MP3 146

Lesson 2 留下聯絡方式

This is my business card.
這是我的名片。

Here is my e-mail address [1].
這是我的電子郵件信箱。

Let me write down [2] your phone number.
讓我寫下你的電話號碼。

Do you have a cellular phone?
你有手機嗎？

How do I contact [3] you?
我要如何聯絡你？

May I have your MSN account [4]?
可以給我你的MSN帳號嗎？

When can I contact you?
我什麼時候可以聯絡你？

Call me anytime you want.
你可以隨時打電話給我。

Phrase List

★**write down** 寫下、記下

Would you write it down for me?

可以幫我寫下來嗎？

★**contact sbdy.** 聯絡某人

I'll contact her by e-mail.

我會用電子郵件和她聯絡。

Phrase List

Word Bank

1. **e-mail address** 電子郵件信箱
2. **write down** 寫下
3. **contact** *v.* 聯絡
4. **account** **n.** 帳號

Word Bank

MP3 147

Lesson 3

保持聯絡

You'll stay in touch, won't you?
你會保持聯絡吧？

Give me a call when you're in Taipei.
如果你來台北，打個電話給我。

Call me when you arrive in Taiwan.
到台灣時打個電話給我。

Let's keep in touch [1].
保持聯絡。

你也可以這麼說：
◆We'll keep in touch.
我們要保持聯絡！

Write me sometime.
有空寫信給我。

Meet you on line.
線上再見囉！

Phrase List

★**stay in touch** 保持聯絡

We'll stay in touch.

我們會保持聯絡。

★**keep in touch** 保持聯絡

Remember to keep in touch.

記得要保持聯絡。

★**write sbdy.** 寫信給某人

I always write my parents on holidays.

假期時我都會寫信給我的父母。

Phrase List

Word Bank

1. keep in touch 保持聯絡

Word Bank

MP3 148

Lesson 4

約定下次訪問

If you're ever in Taipei again, you must look me up[1].

如果你來台北，一定要來拜訪我。

I hope we'll meet again soon.

我希望我們不久能夠再見面。

Hope to see you again soon.

希望很快再見到你。

I can't wait to see you again.

我等不及再看到你。

Let's get together again soon.

我們盡快再找個時間聚一聚。

When will you come again?

你什麼時候要再來？

I hope to visit your country sometime.

我希望有空去拜訪你的國家。

I'd like to drop in[2] and see you sometime next week.

我想在下週順便去看看你。

Phrase List

★**look up** 拜訪某人

Remember to look me up.

記得要來拜訪我。

★**drop in** 拜訪

I drop in and check these out when I can.

如果可以，我去拜訪並確定這些事。

Word Bank

1. look up 拜訪

2. drop in 拜訪

MP3 149

Lesson 5

客套用語

Well done.

幹得好！

你也可以這麼說：

◆Good job.

幹得好！

Thank you so much.

非常感謝。

Thanks for all your help this week.

感謝你們這一週來的協助。

Thank you to you and your staff.

謝謝你和你的工作人員。

You are so nice to me.

你對我真好。

It's a pleasure to meet you.

很高興認識你。

Phrase List

★**well done** 表現傑出

Well done, Jonny.

強尼，幹得好！

★**good job** 表現優秀

You've done a good job.

你表現得很優秀。

★**someone's pleasure to**+原形動詞 某人的榮幸去做某事

It's my pleasure to serve you.

很高興能為您服務。

MP3 150

Lesson 6

祝福用語

Have a safe trip.
祝你旅途平安。

Safe flight.
旅途平安！

你也可以這麼說：

◆Safe trip.
旅途平安！

Have a good flight back.
祝你回程旅途平安。

Good luck.
祝你好運。

Take care.
保重。

Take care of yourself, my friend.
我的朋友，請保重。

Please say hello to Mr. White for me.

請幫我向懷特先生打招呼。

Phrase List

★take care of 照顧、保重

You take care of yourself.

你要好好保重自己。

Would you take care of my job?

你能幫我處理我的工作嗎？

★**say hello** 打招呼

Tell your boss I say hello to him.

幫我向你的老闆打聲招呼。

全民學英文
55

出差英文1000句型

雅致風靡　典藏文化

親愛的顧客您好，感謝您購買這本書。即日起，填寫讀者回函卡寄回至本公司，我們每月將抽出一百名回函讀者，寄出精美禮物並享有生日當月購書優惠！想知道更多更即時的消息，歡迎加入"永續圖書粉絲團"
您也可以選擇傳真、掃描或用本公司準備的免郵回函寄回，謝謝。

傳真電話：（02）8647-3660　　電子信箱：yungjiuh@ms45.hinet.net

姓名：	性別：　□男　□女
出生日期：　年　月　日	電話：
學歷：	職業：
E-mail：	
地址：□□□	
從何處購買此書：	購買金額：　元
購買本書動機：□封面 □書名 □排版 □內容 □作者 □偶然衝動	
你對本書的意見： 內容：□滿意□尚可□待改進 封面：□滿意□尚可□待改進	編輯：□滿意□尚可□待改進 定價：□滿意□尚可□待改進
其他建議：	

您可以使用以下方式將回函寄回。

您的回覆，是我們進步的最大動力，謝謝。

① 使用本公司準備的免郵回函寄回。

② 傳真電話：（02）8647-3660

③ 掃描圖檔寄到電子信箱：

yungjiuh@ms45.hinet.net

沿此線對折後寄回，謝謝。

廣 告 回 信
基隆郵局登記證
基隆廣字第056號

221-03

雅典文化事業有限公司　收

新北市汐止區大同路三段194號9樓之1

雅致風靡　典藏文化